MERMAID DAYS™

The Sea Monster

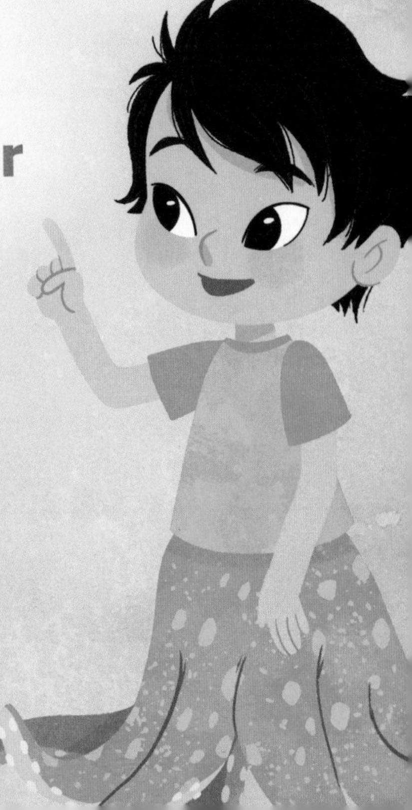

Read more MERMAID DAYS™ books!

MERMAID DAYS™
ACORN
The Sunken Ship
WRITTEN BY
Kyle Lukoff
ART BY
Kat Uno
SCHOLASTIC

MERMAID DAYS™
ACORN
A New Friend
WRITTEN BY
Kyle Lukoff
ART BY
Kat Uno
SCHOLASTIC

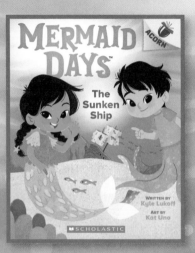

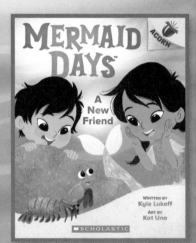

MERMAID DAYS™

The Sea Monster

WRITTEN BY
Kyle Lukoff

ART BY
Kat Uno

🔱 **ACORN**™
SCHOLASTIC INC.

To Alix, who inspired Mr. Burbles.
—**KL**

To my family, thank you for giving me the motivation to work towards my dreams.
—**KU**

Text copyright © 2022 by Kyle Lukoff.
Illustrations copyright © 2022 by Kat Uno.

Library of Congress Cataloging-in-Publication Data Available

Names: Lukoff, Kyle, author. | Uno, Kat, illustrator.
Title: The sea monster / by Kyle Lukoff ; illustrated by Kat Uno.
Description: First edition. | New York : Acorn/Scholastic Inc., 2022. |
Series: Mermaid days ; 2 | Audience: Ages 5–7. | Audience: Grades K–1. |
Summary: Vera the mermaid and her half-octopus friend Beaker meet a friendly kraken on a field trip.
Identifiers: LCCN 2021045095 | ISBN 9781338794656 (paperback) |
ISBN 9781338794687 (hardcover)
Subjects: LCSH: Mermaids—Juvenile fiction. | Kraken—Juvenile fiction. |
Marine animals—Juvenile fiction. | CYAC: Mermaids—Fiction. |
Kraken—Fiction. | Marine animals—Fiction. | LCGFT: Picture books.
Classification: LCC PZ7.1.L8456 Se 2022 | DDC [E]—dc23
LC record available at https://lccn.loc.gov/2021045095

10 9 8 7 6 5 4 3 2 1   22 23 24 25 26

Printed in China   62
First edition, September 2022
Edited by Rachel Matson
Designed by Jaime Lucero

TABLE OF CONTENTS

On the Shore 1

The Sea Monster 18

The Visitor 40

WHO LIVES IN TIDAL GROVE?

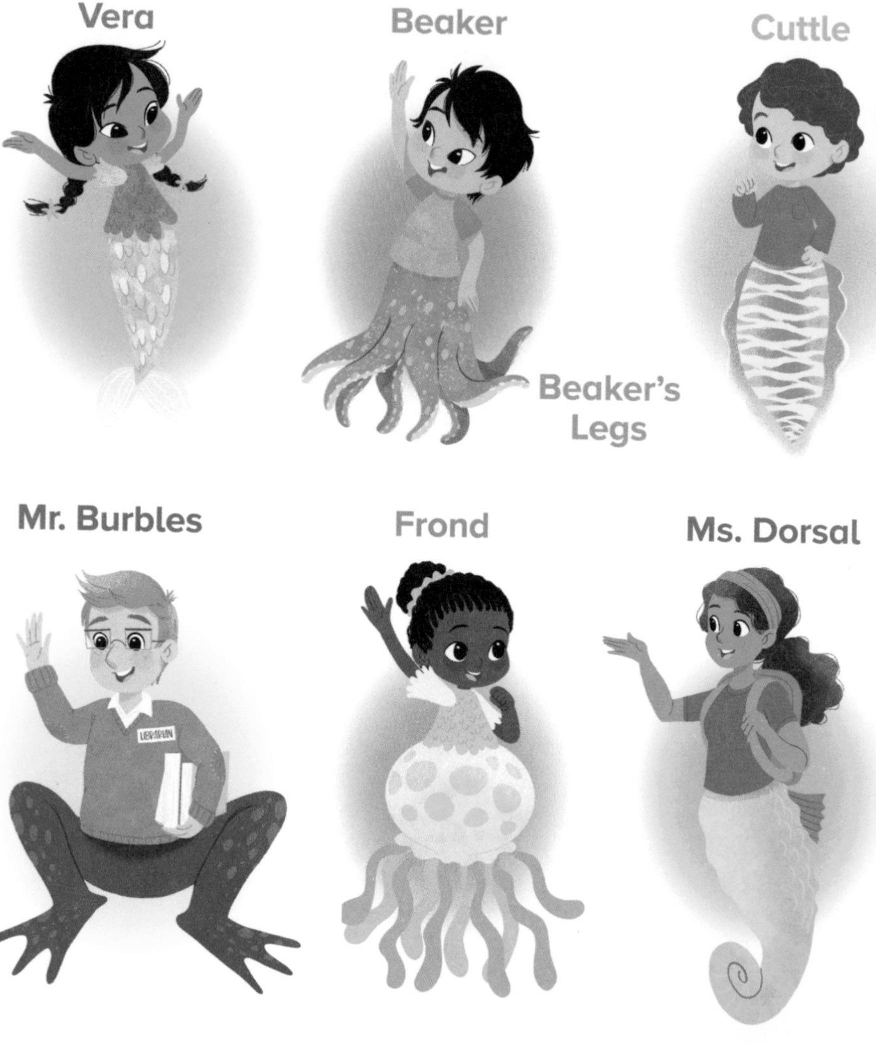

Vera
Beaker
Cuttle
Beaker's Legs
Mr. Burbles
LIBRARIAN
Frond
Ms. Dorsal

ON THE SHORE

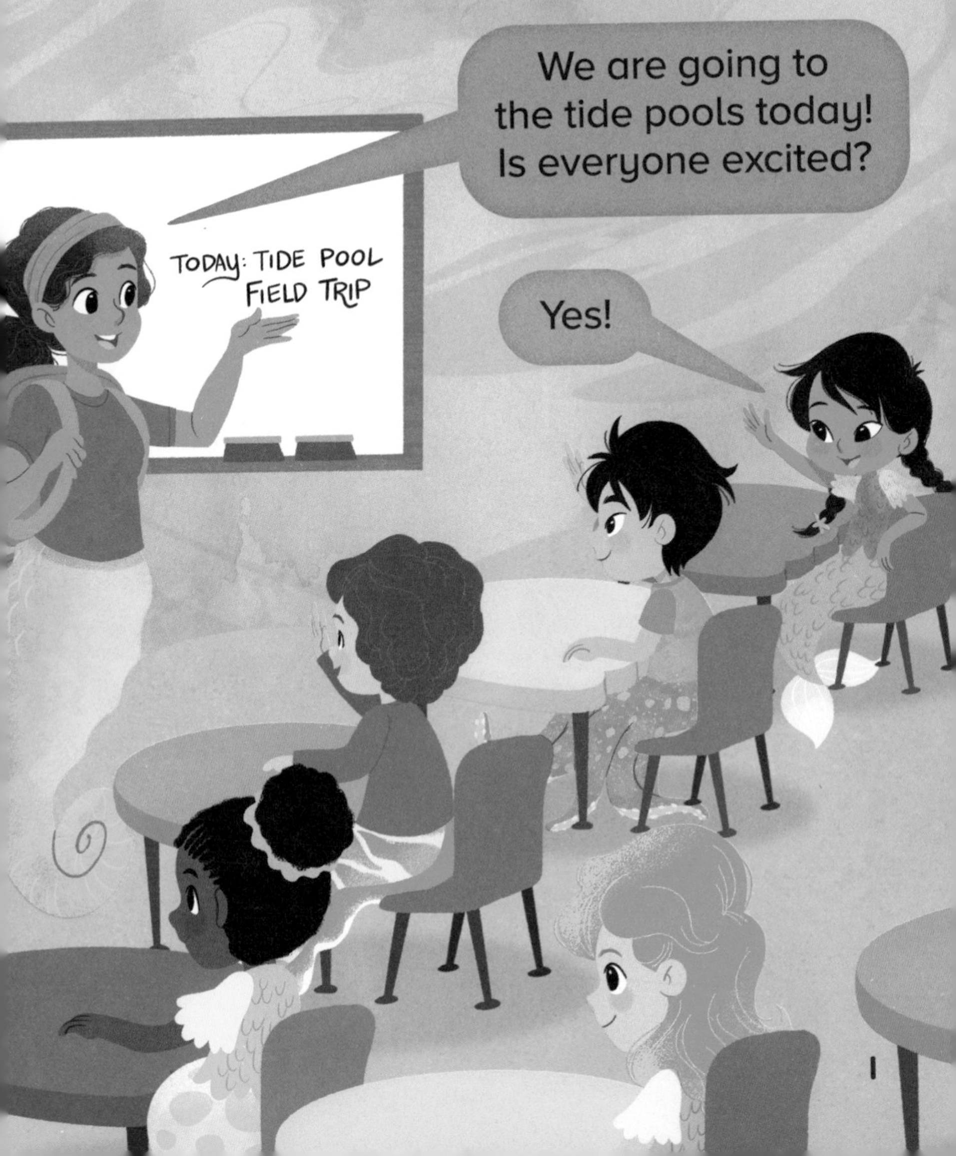
We are going to the tide pools today! Is everyone excited?
TODAY: TIDE POOL FIELD TRIP
Yes!

DID YOU KNOW?

Tide pools are shallow pools of seawater. You can find them where the ocean meets the land!

Tide pools are home to all sorts of plants and animals.

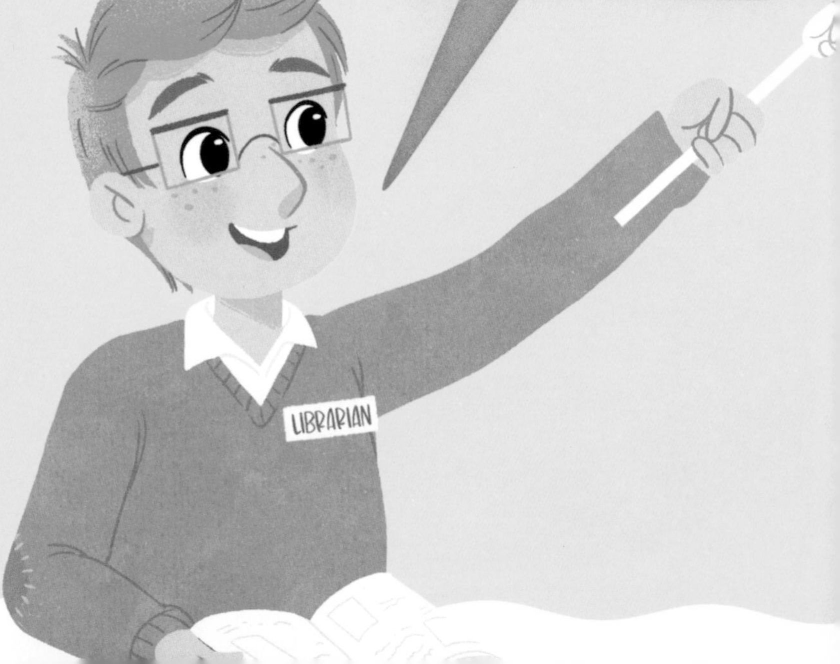
LIBRARIAN

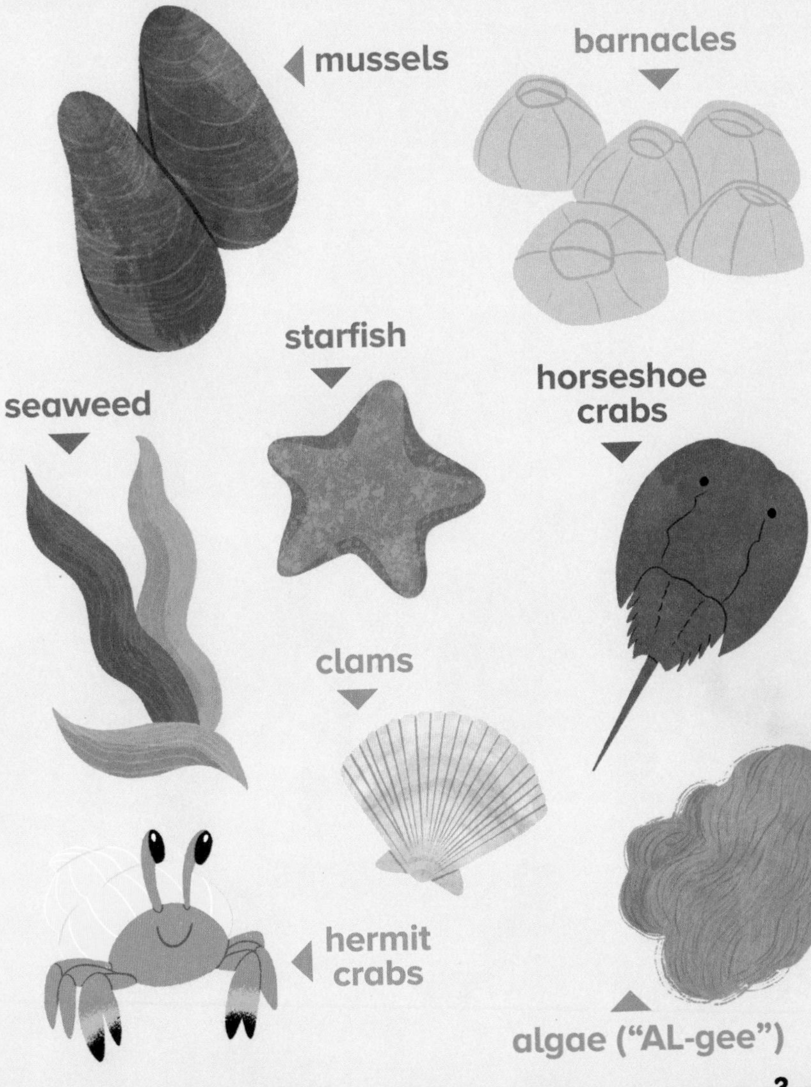
mussels
barnacles
starfish
seaweed
horseshoe crabs
clams
hermit crabs
algae ("AL-gee")

I love field trips with Ms. Dorsal!
Me too!
I've never been to the tide pools before. I want to play with a hermit crab.
I want to pet a starfish!

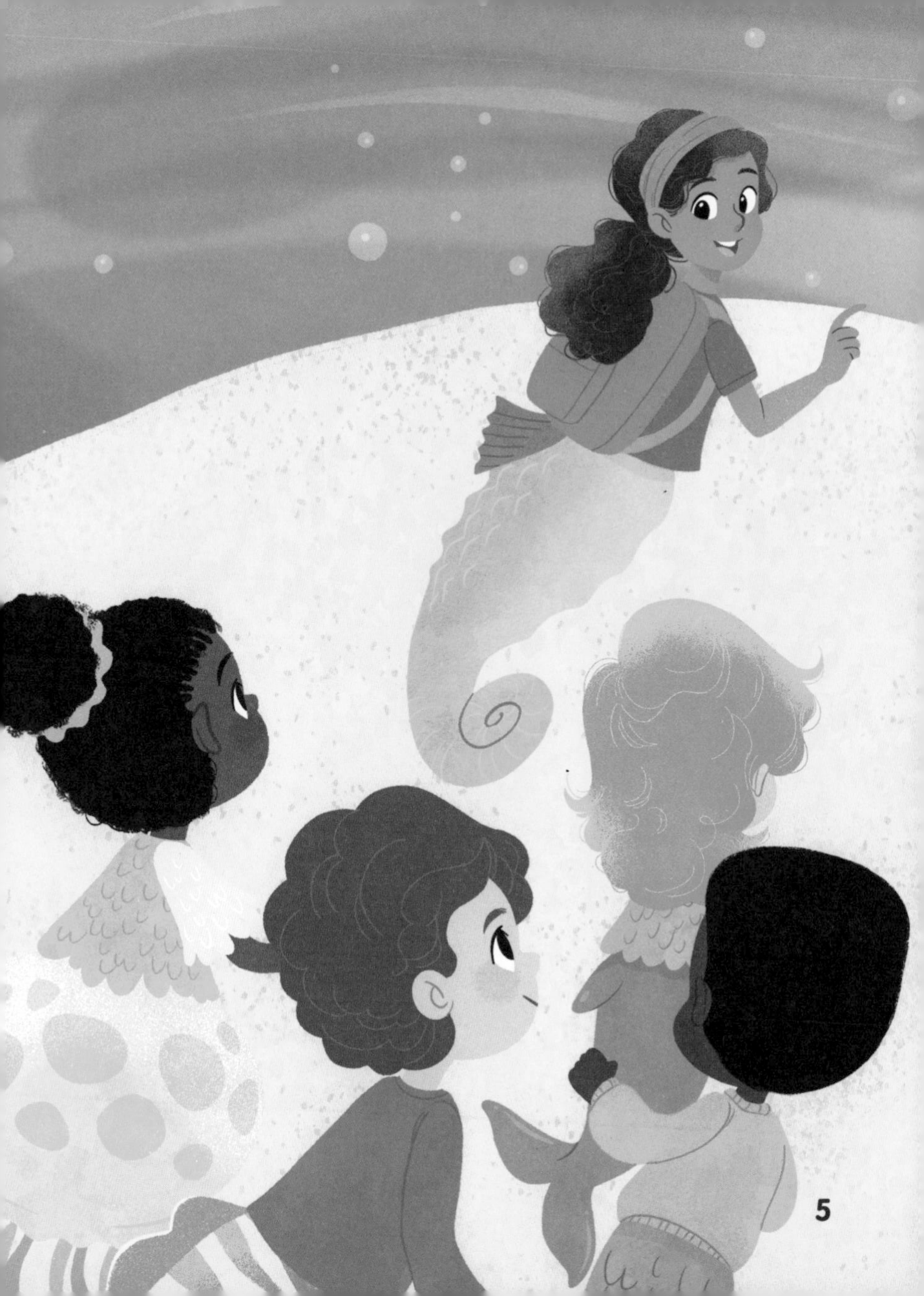

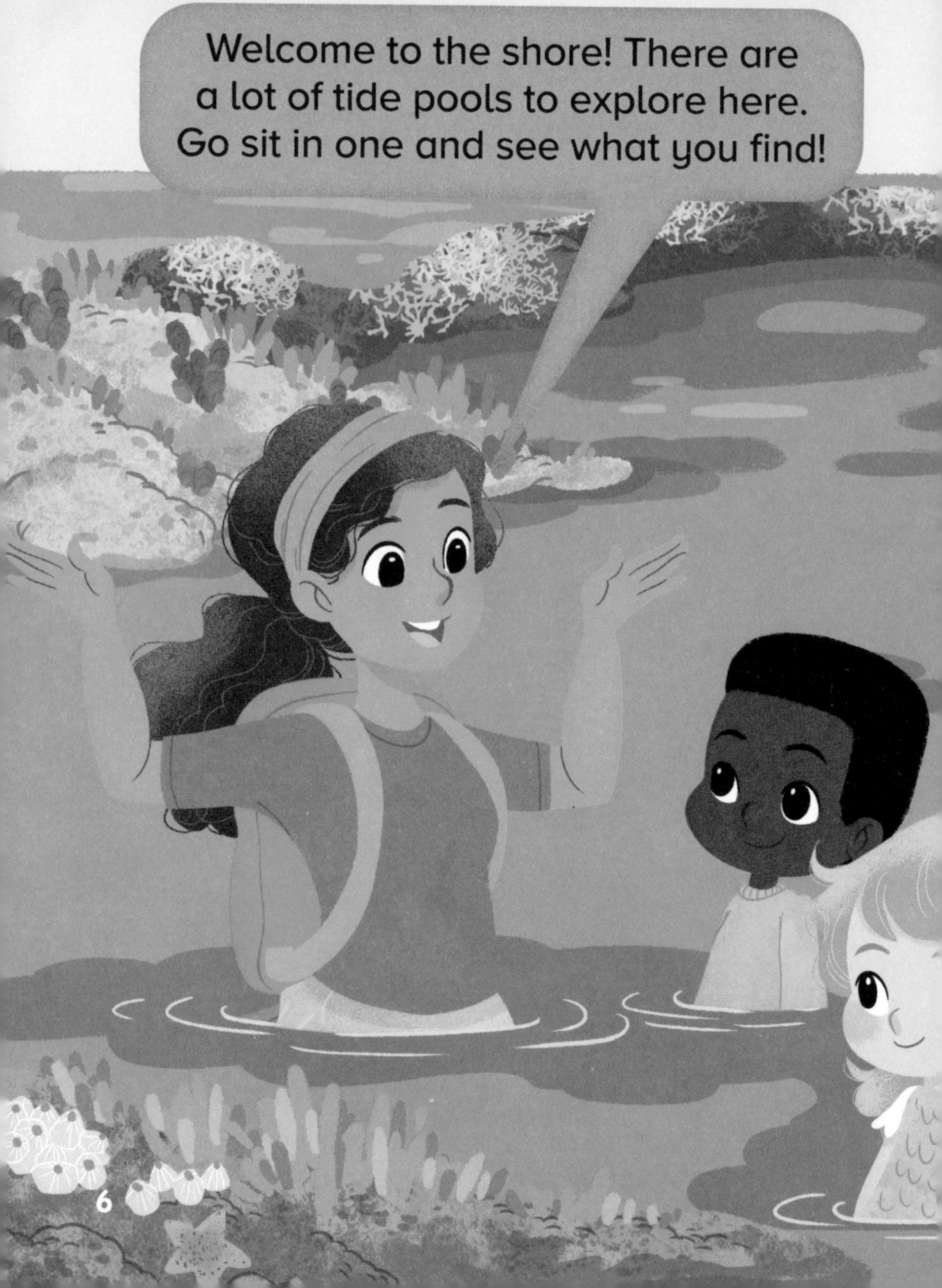
Welcome to the shore! There are a lot of tide pools to explore here. Go sit in one and see what you find!

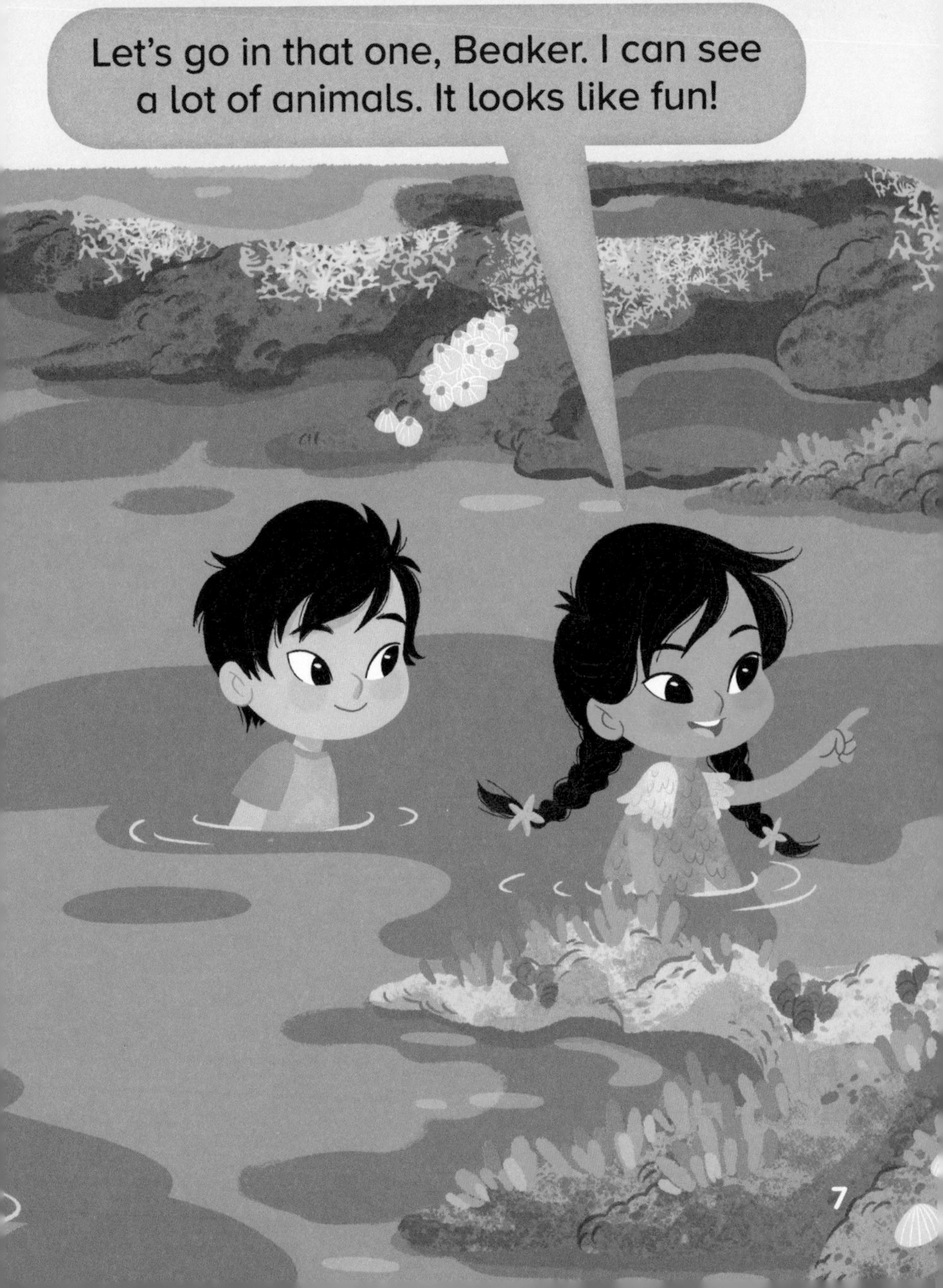
Let's go in that one, Beaker. I can see a lot of animals. It looks like fun!

Ooh, the water is nice and warm.
But I don't see any animals. Where did they go?

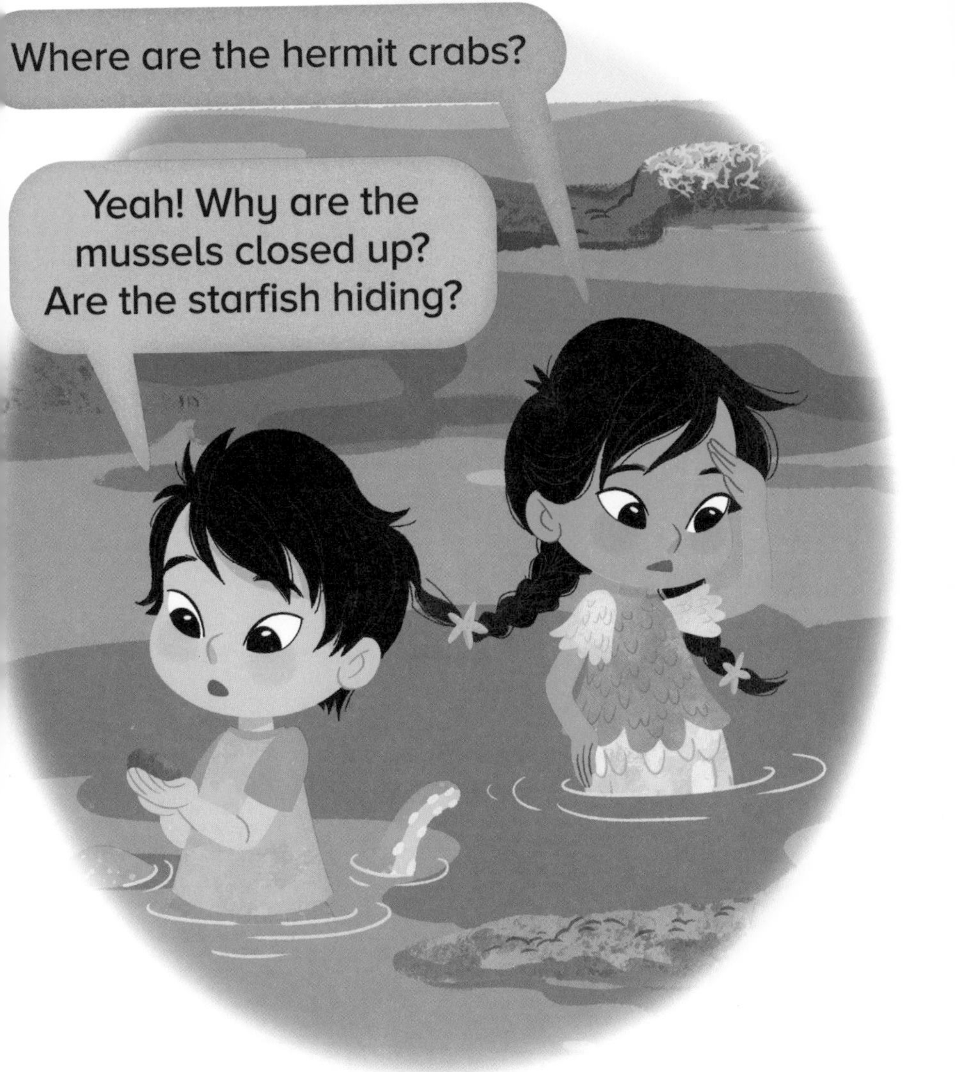
Where are the hermit crabs?
Yeah! Why are the mussels closed up? Are the starfish hiding?

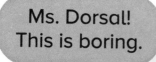

Ms. Dorsal!
This is boring.

We want to see the
animals in the tide pool.

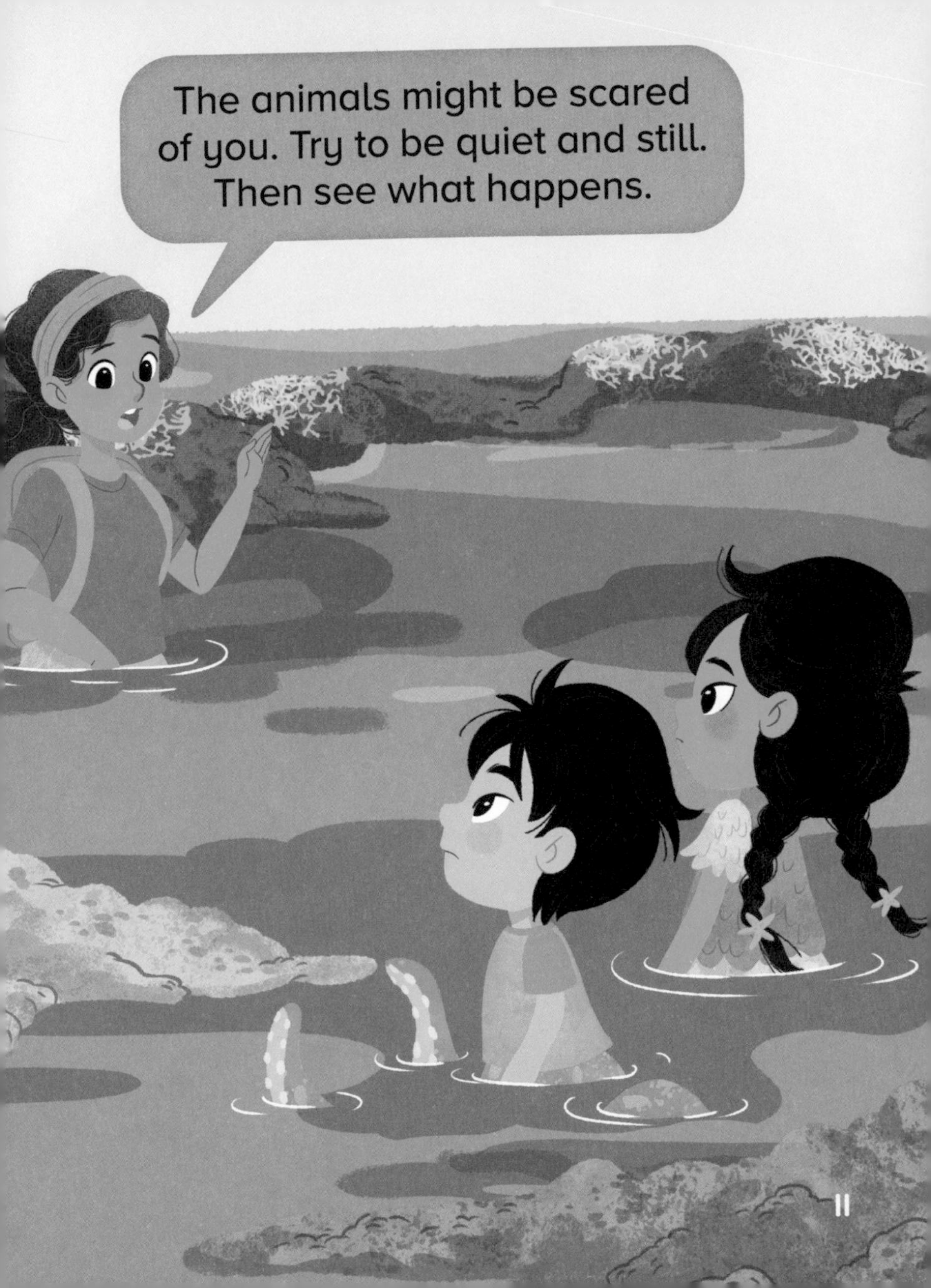
The animals might be scared of you. Try to be quiet and still. Then see what happens.

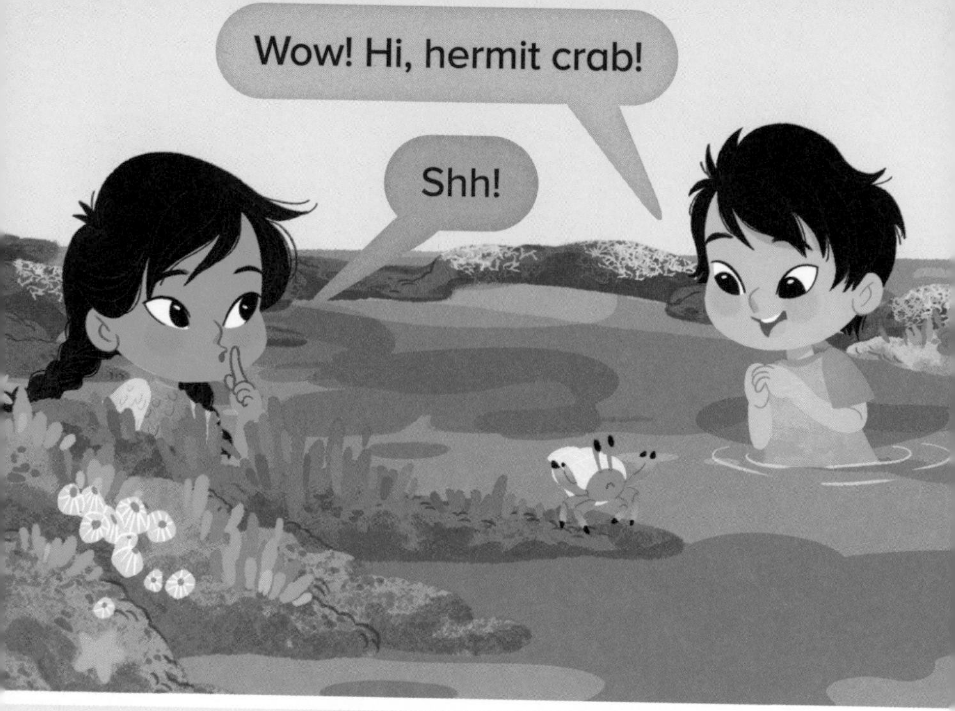
Wow! Hi, hermit crab!
Shh!

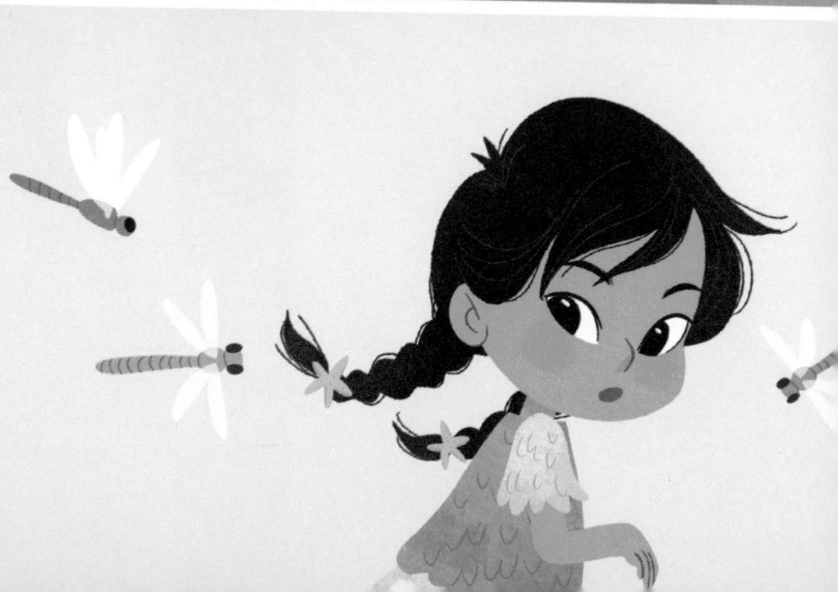

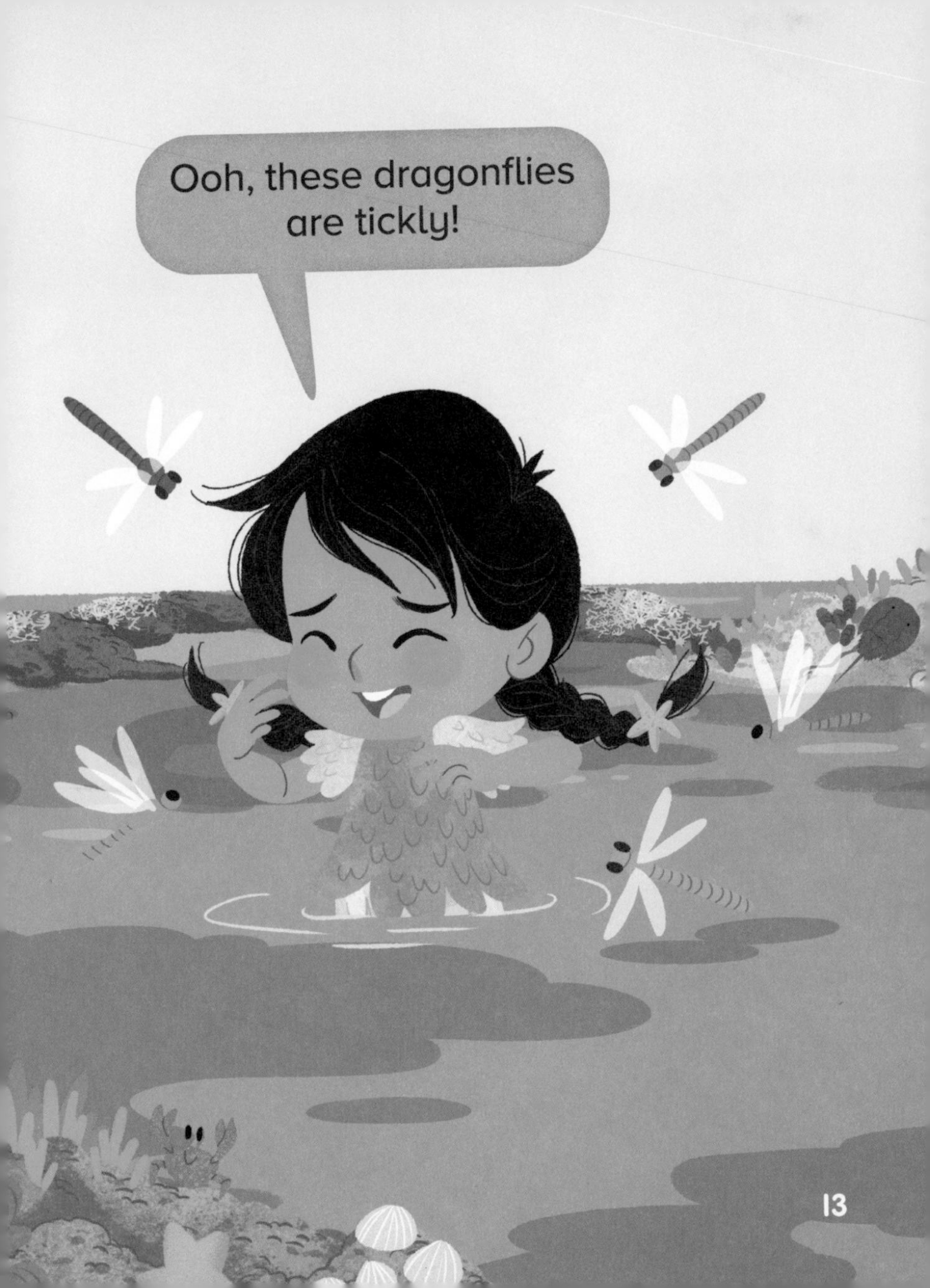
Ooh, these dragonflies are tickly!

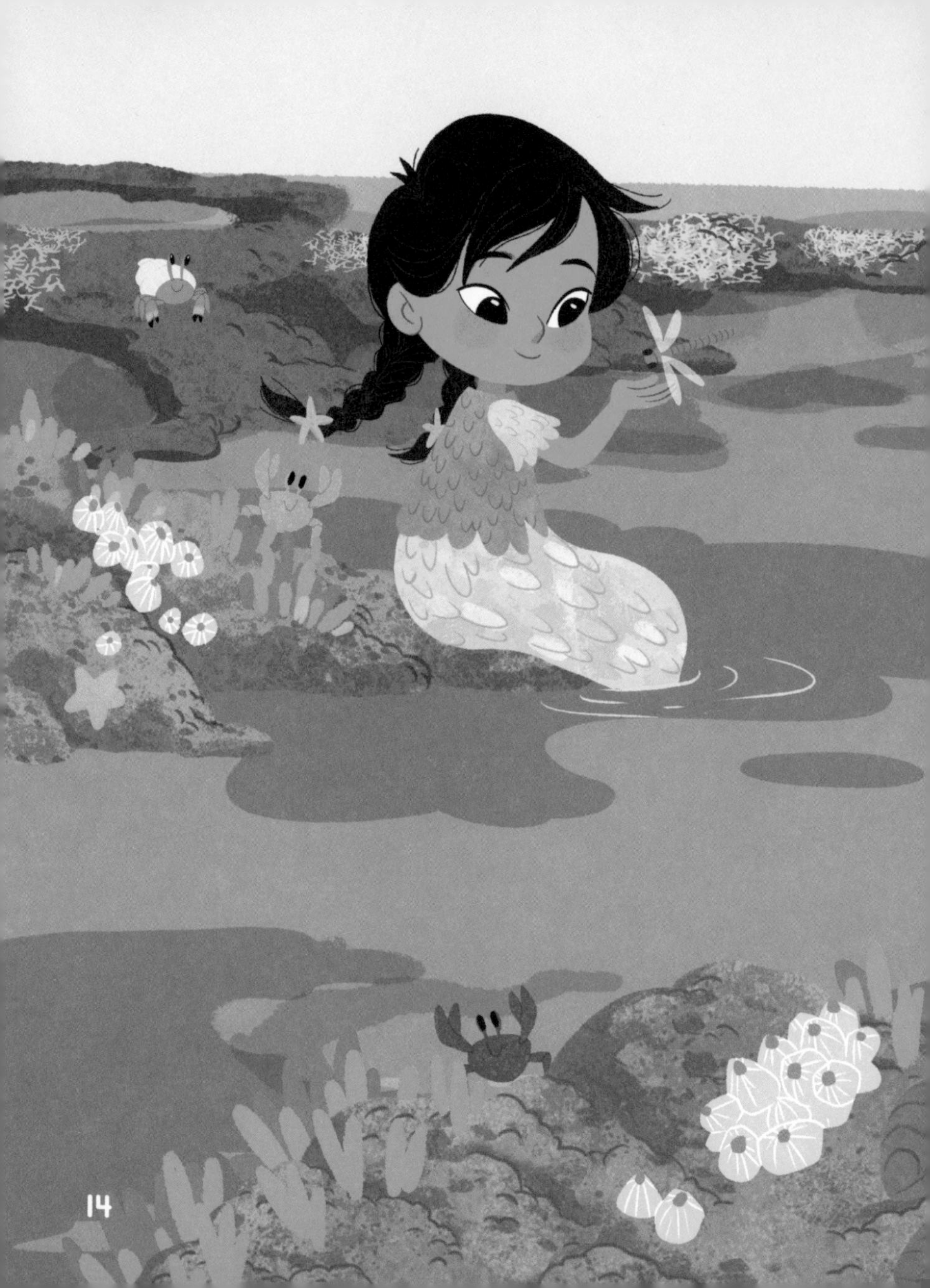

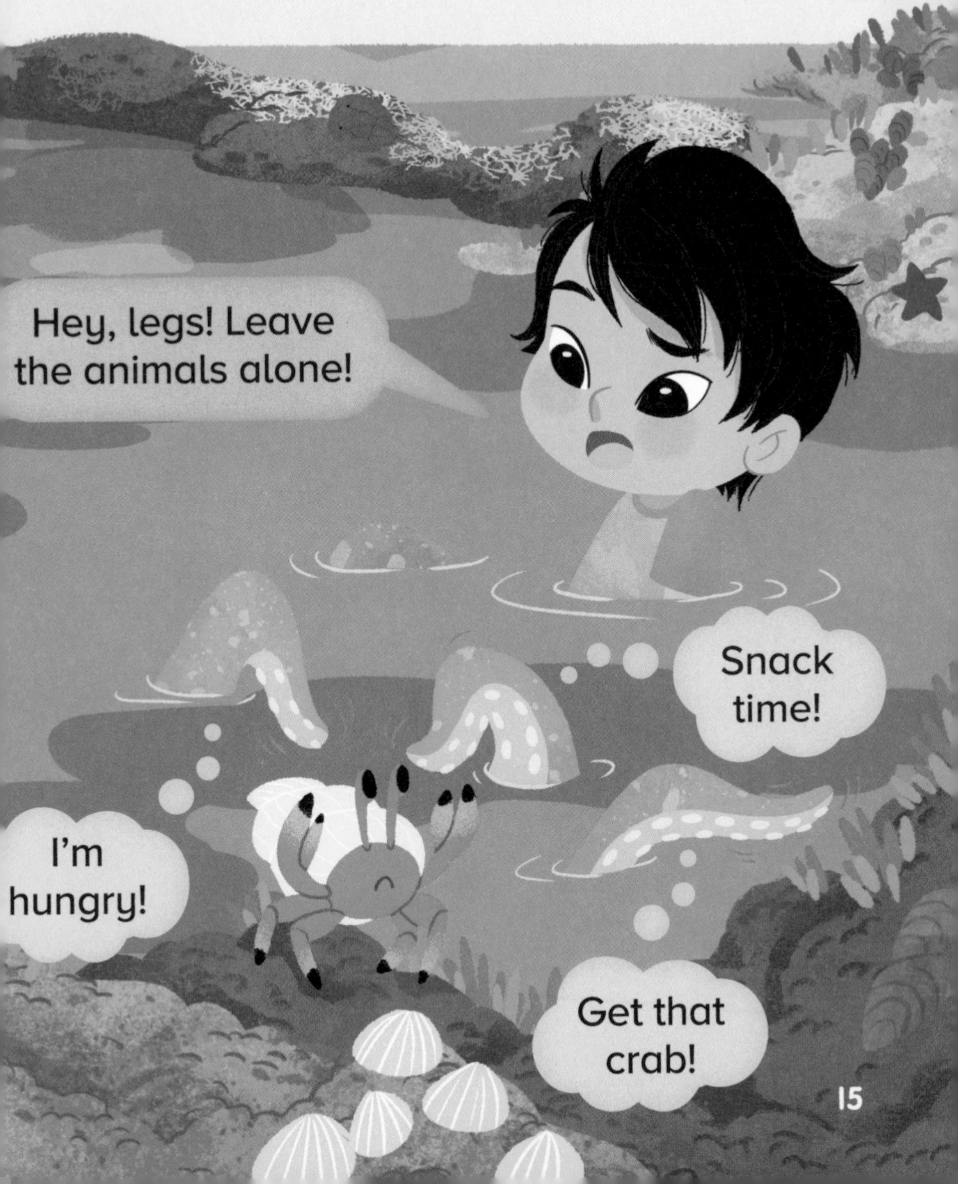
Hey, legs! Leave the animals alone!
Snack time!
I'm hungry!
Get that crab!

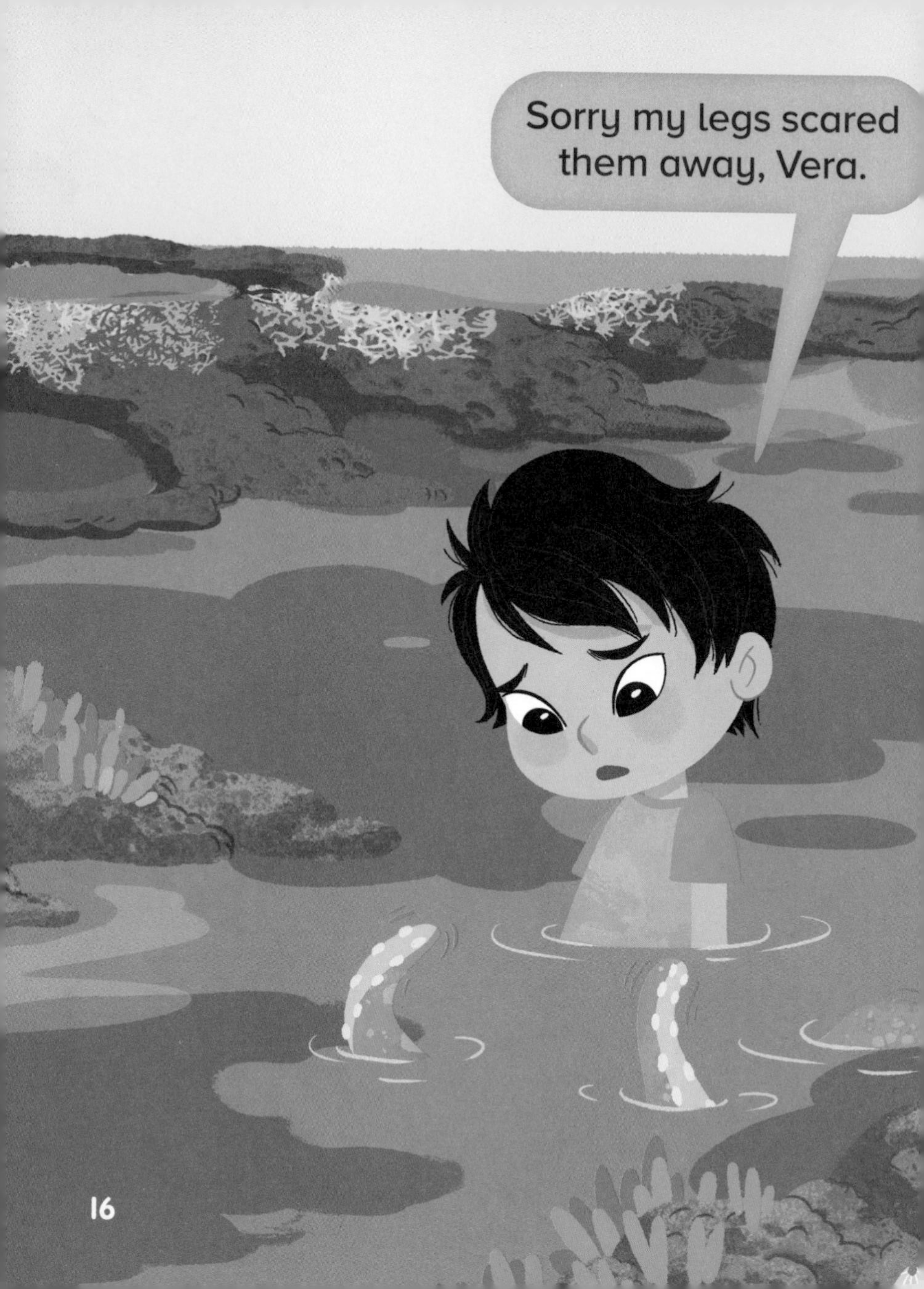
Sorry my legs scared them away, Vera.

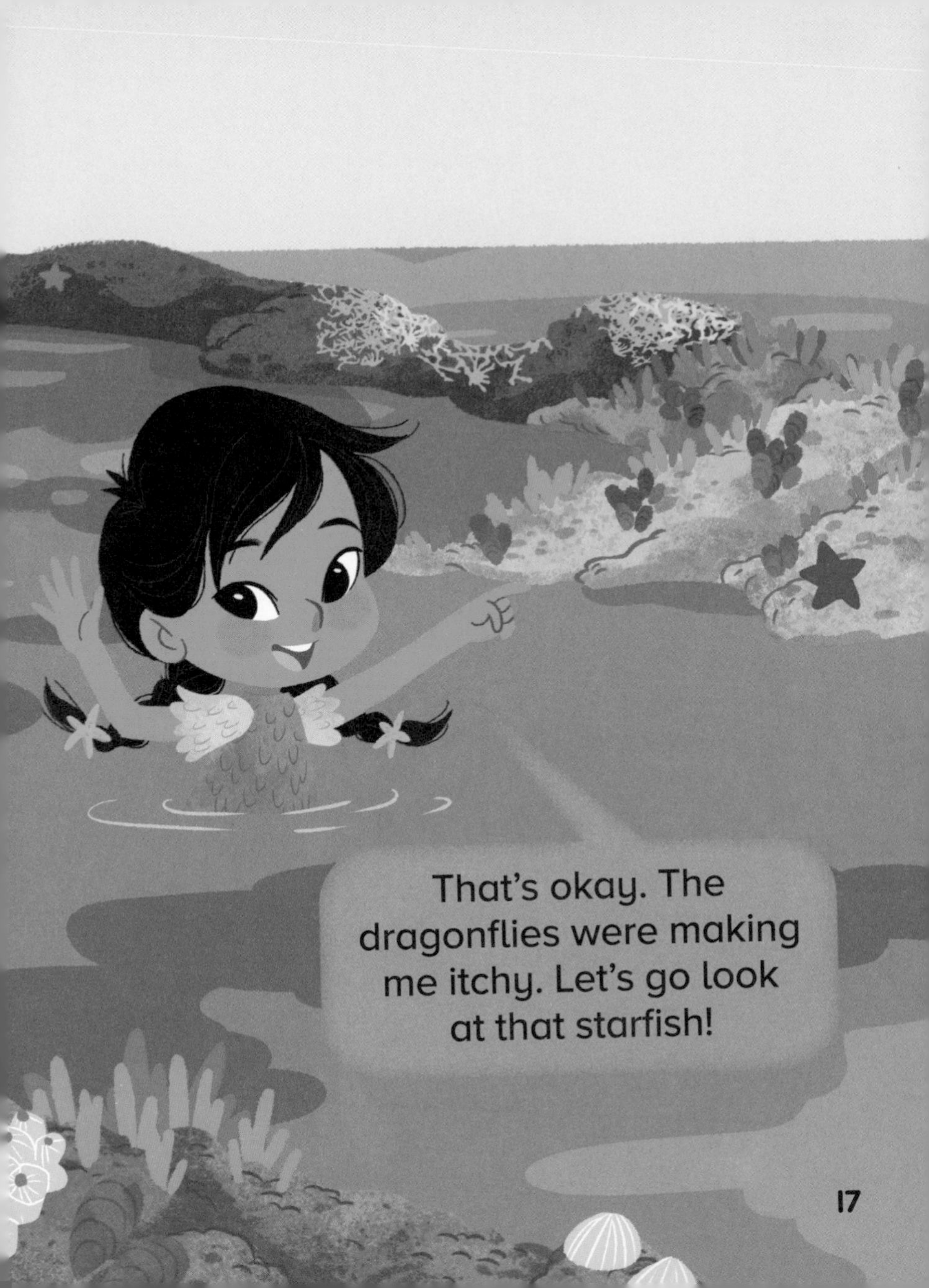
That's okay. The dragonflies were making me itchy. Let's go look at that starfish!

THE SEA MONSTER

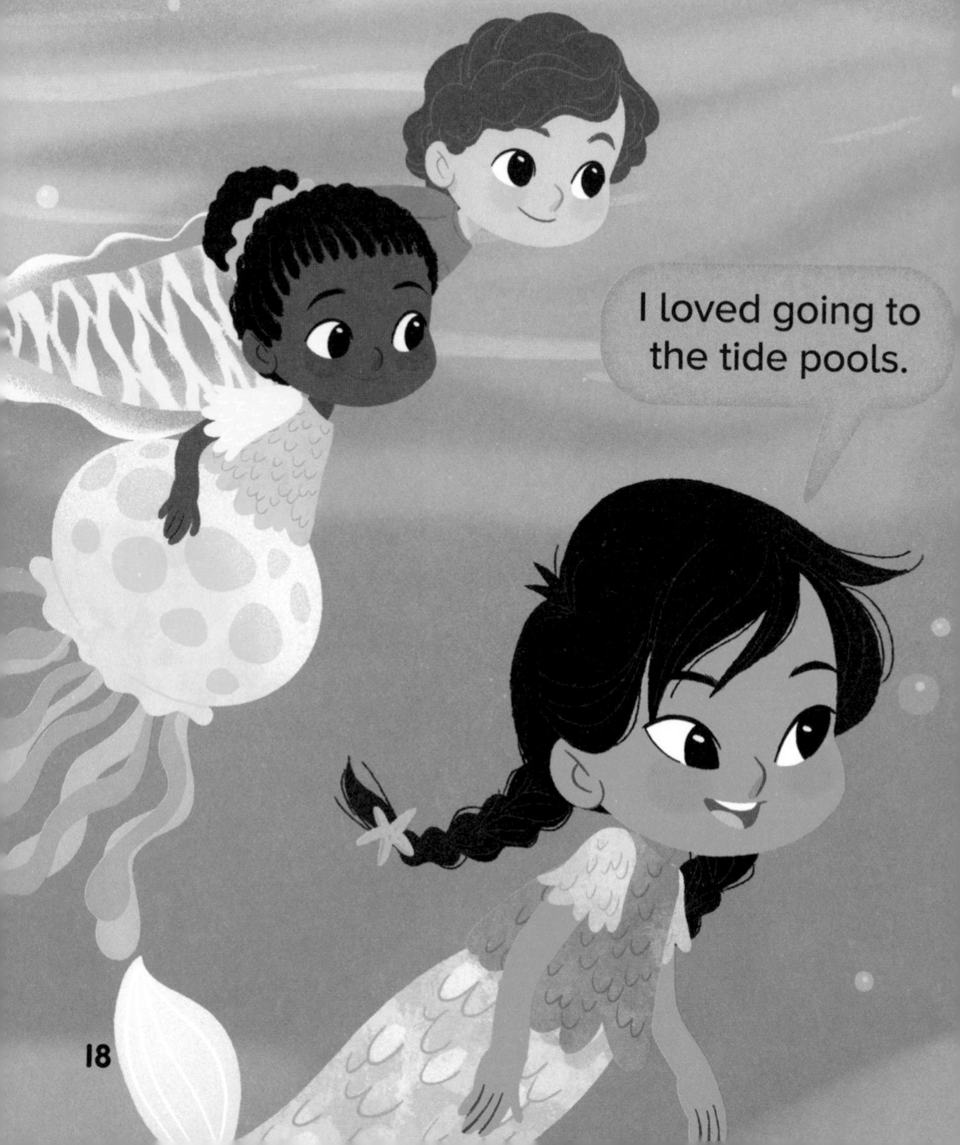
I loved going to the tide pools.

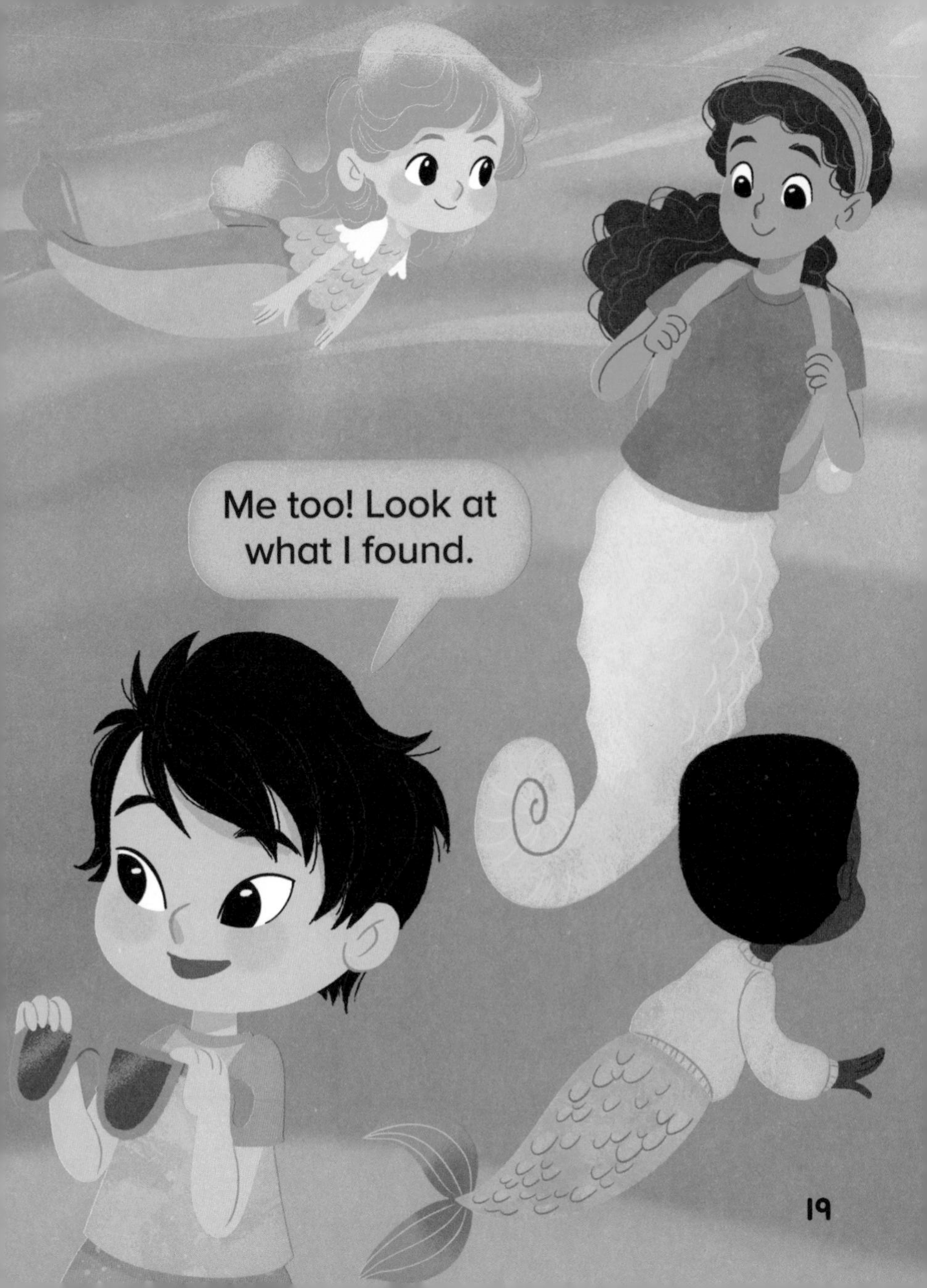
Me too! Look at what I found.

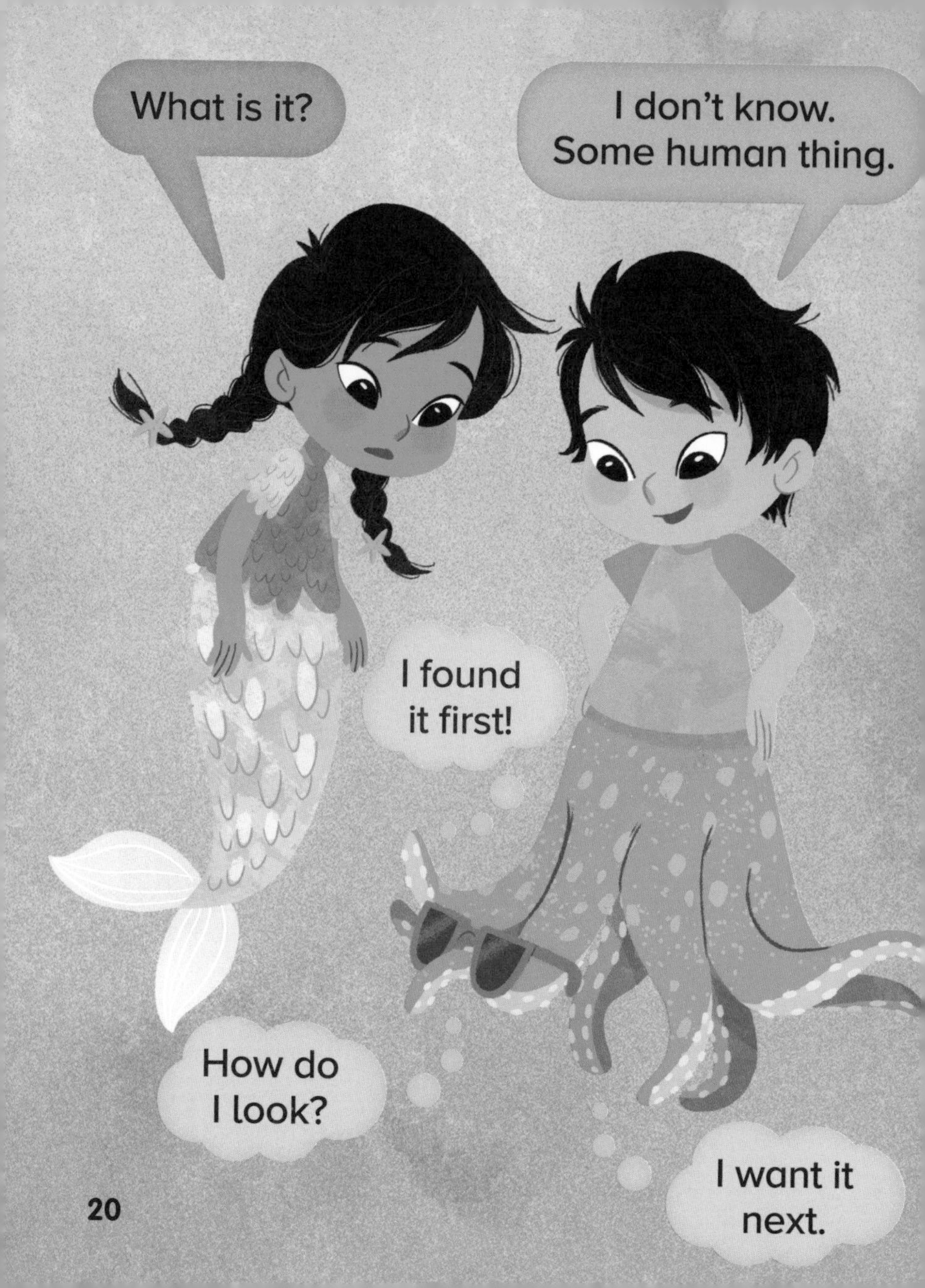
What is it?
I don't know. Some human thing.
I found it first!
How do I look?
I want it next.

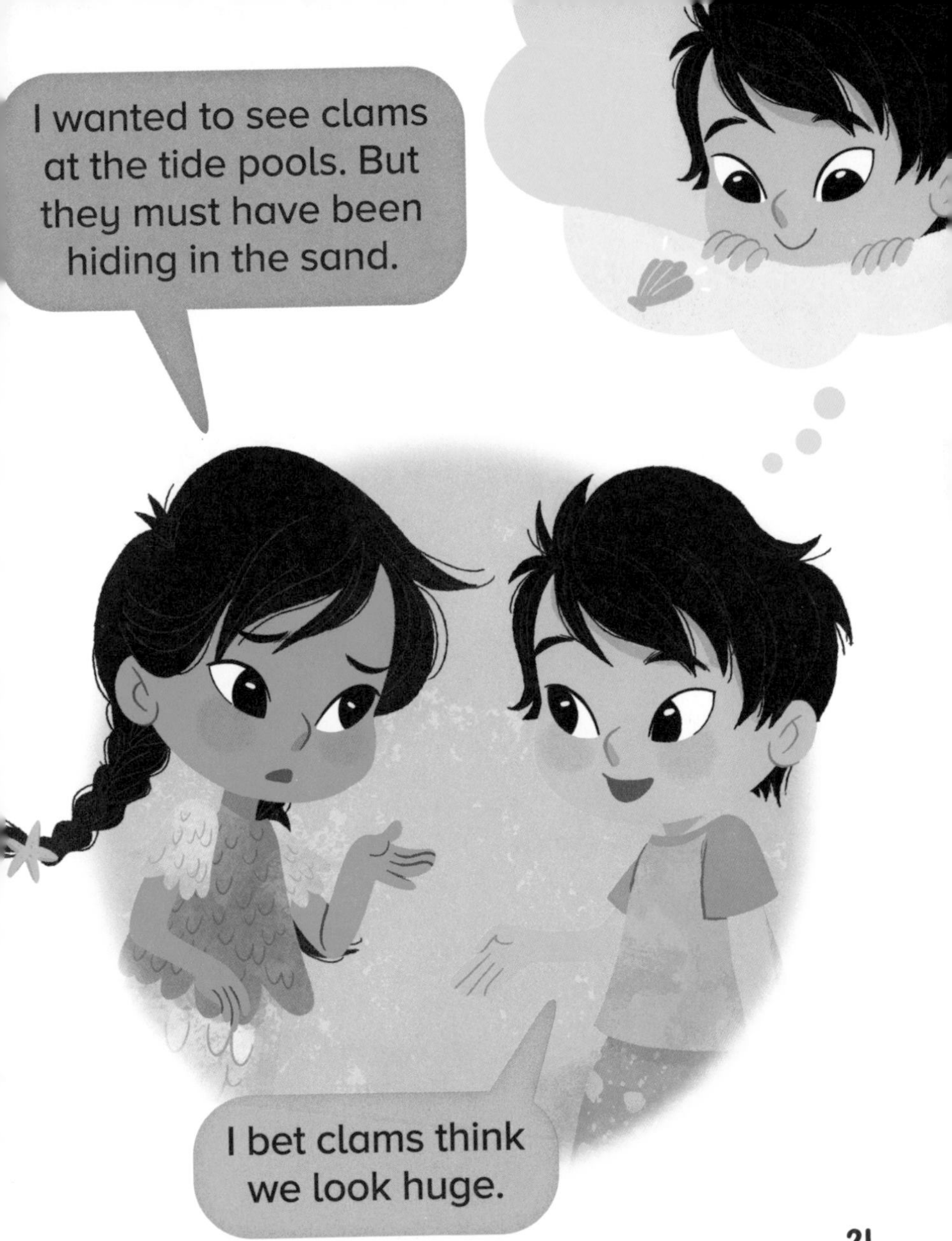
I wanted to see clams at the tide pools. But they must have been hiding in the sand.
I bet clams think we look huge.

But we aren't huge!

Do you think giant squids think we look tiny?

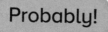
Probably!

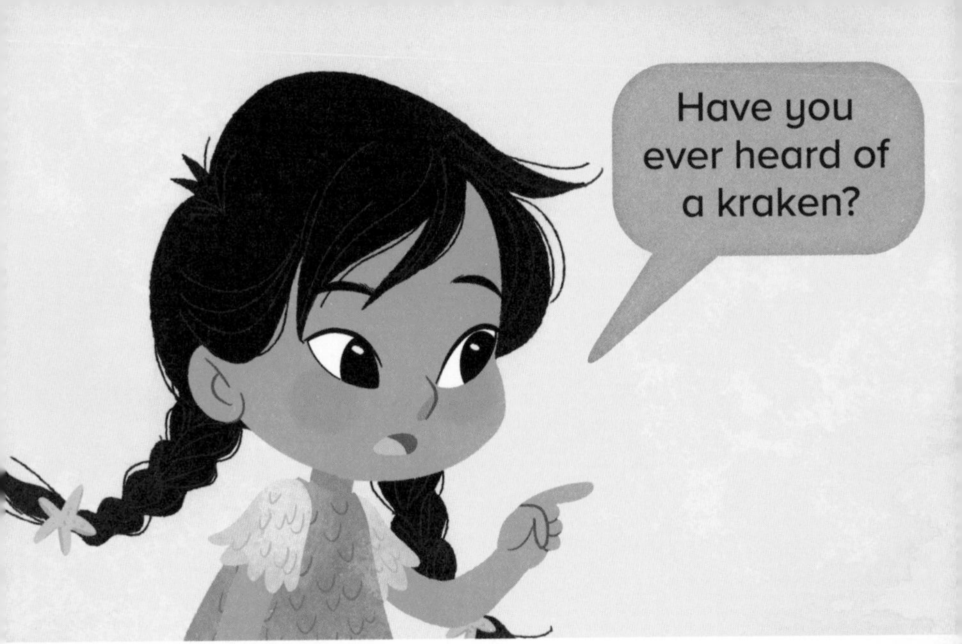
Have you ever heard of a kraken?

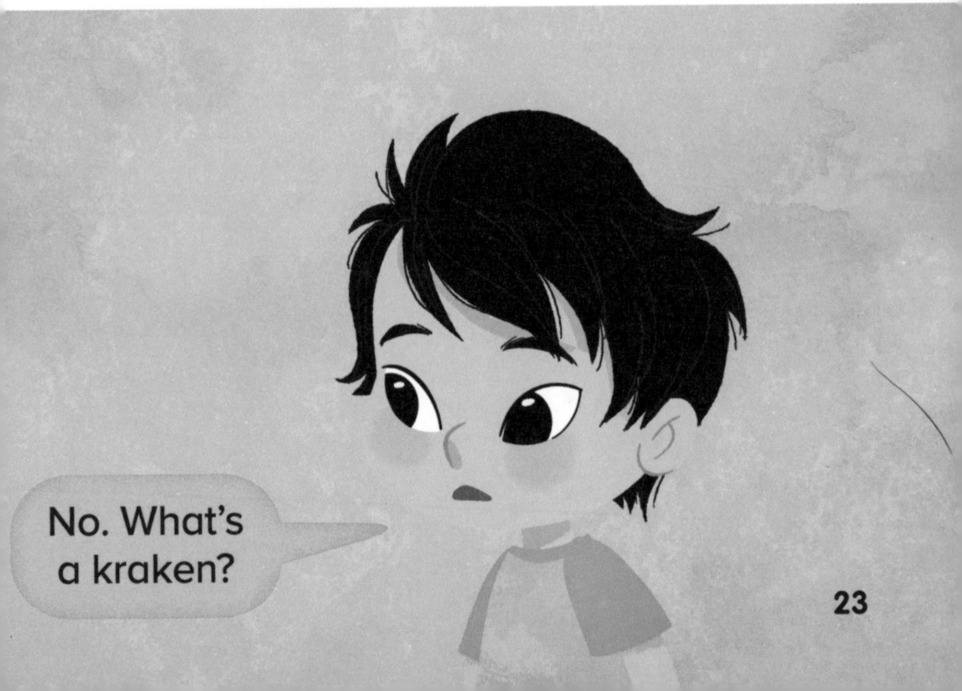
No. What's a kraken?

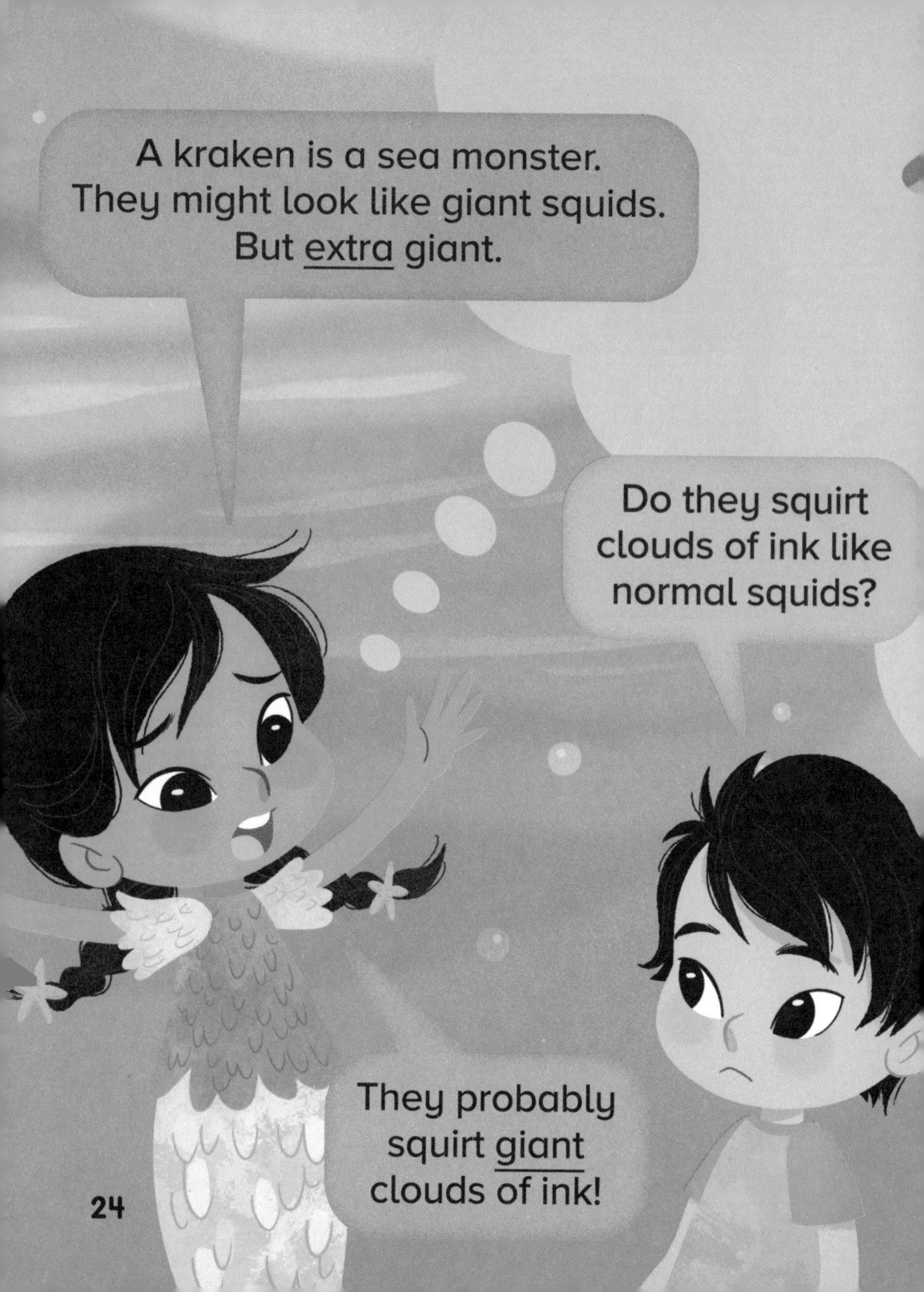
A kraken is a sea monster. They might look like giant squids. But extra giant.
Do they squirt clouds of ink like normal squids?
They probably squirt giant clouds of ink!

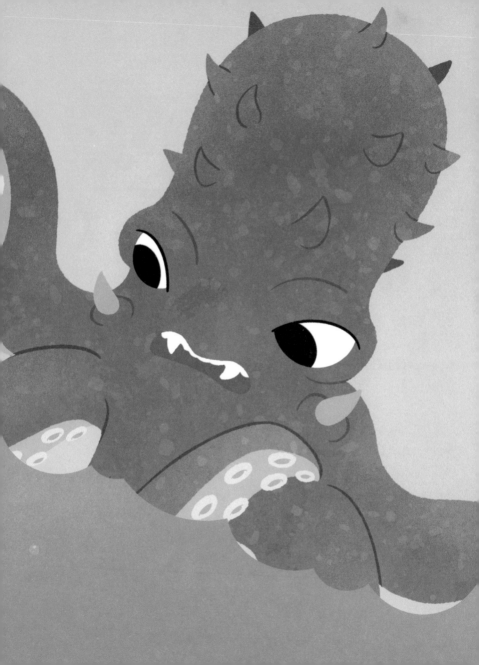

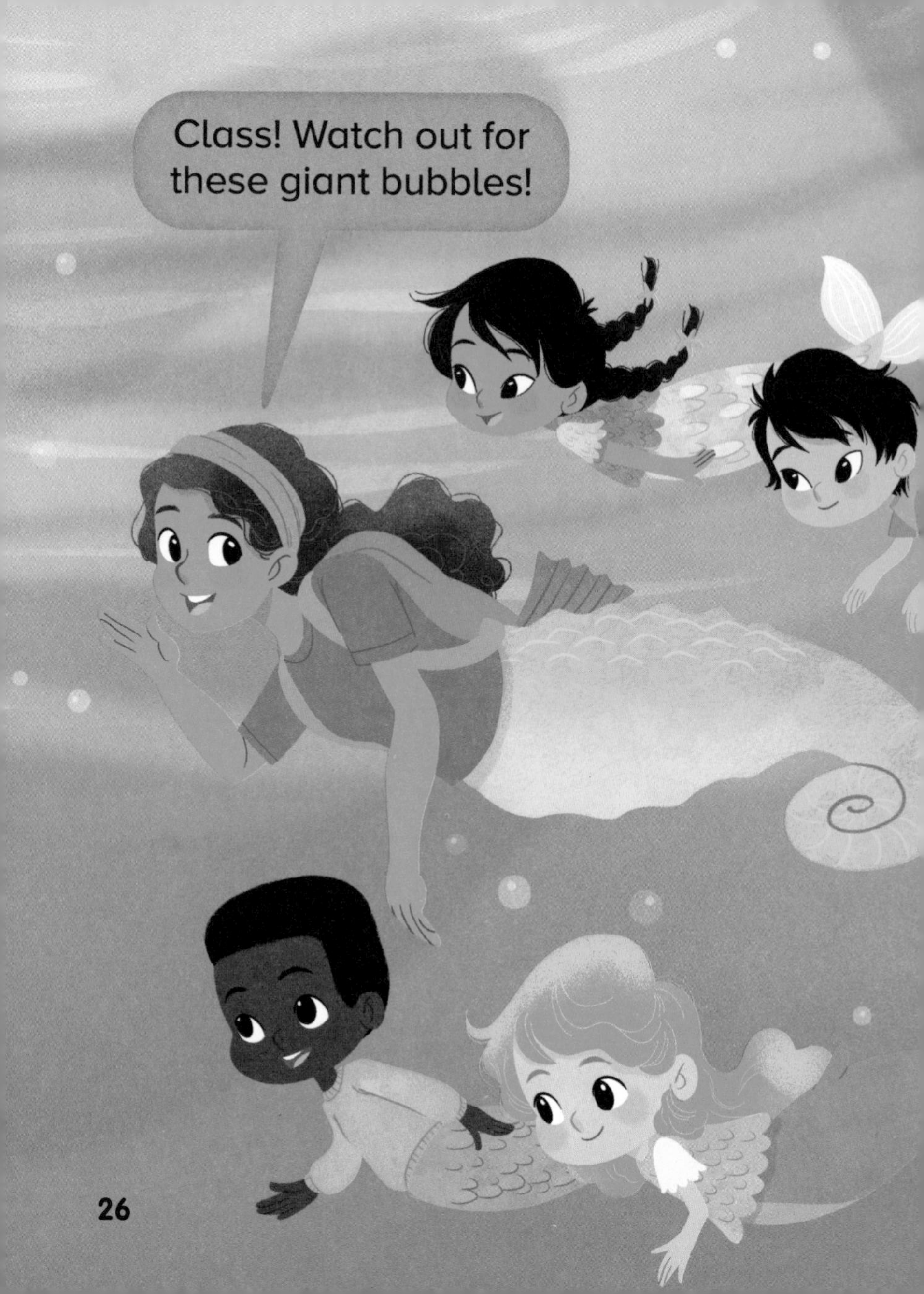
Class! Watch out for these giant bubbles!

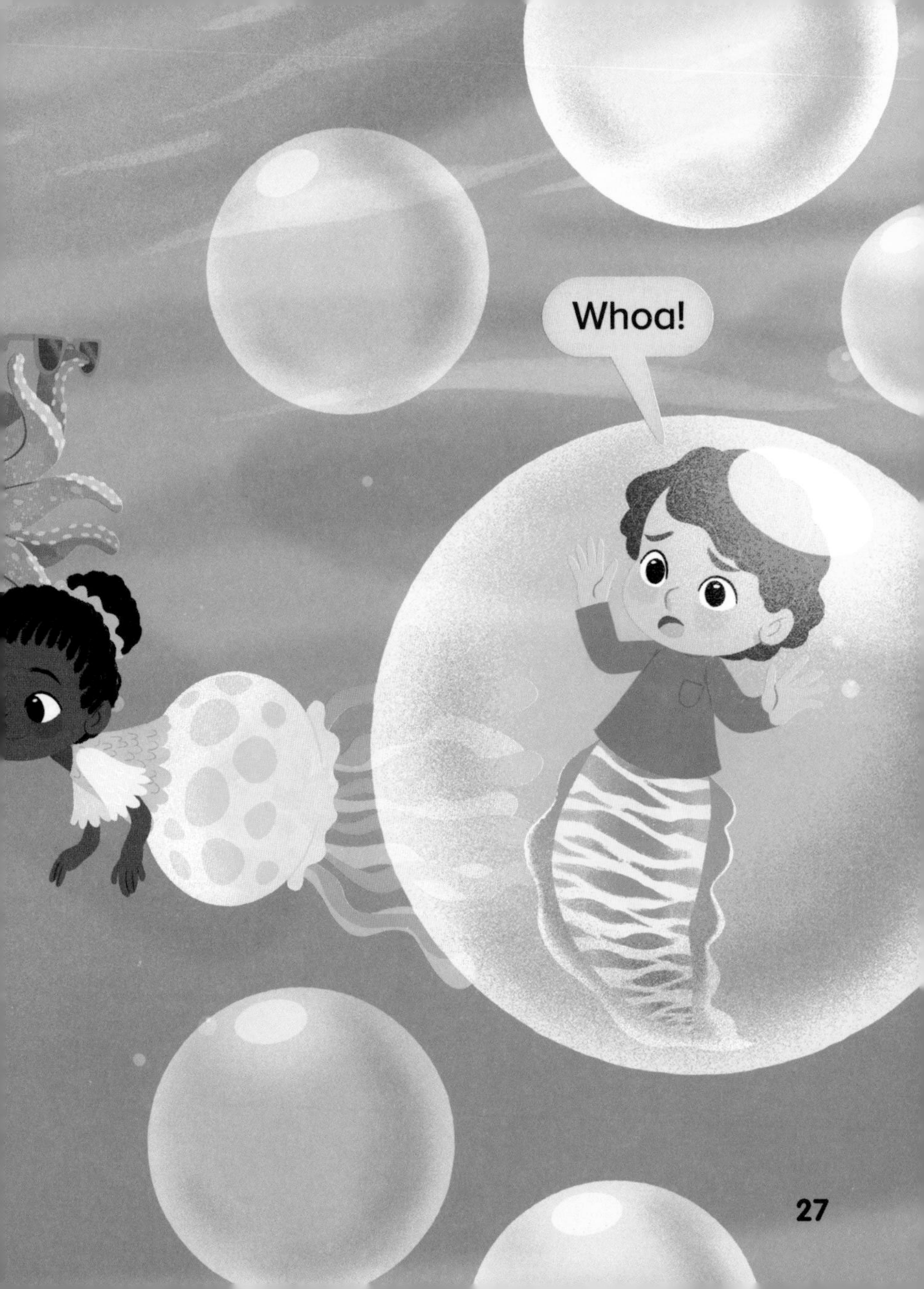
Whoa!

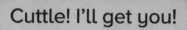

Cuttle! I'll get you!

pop!

28

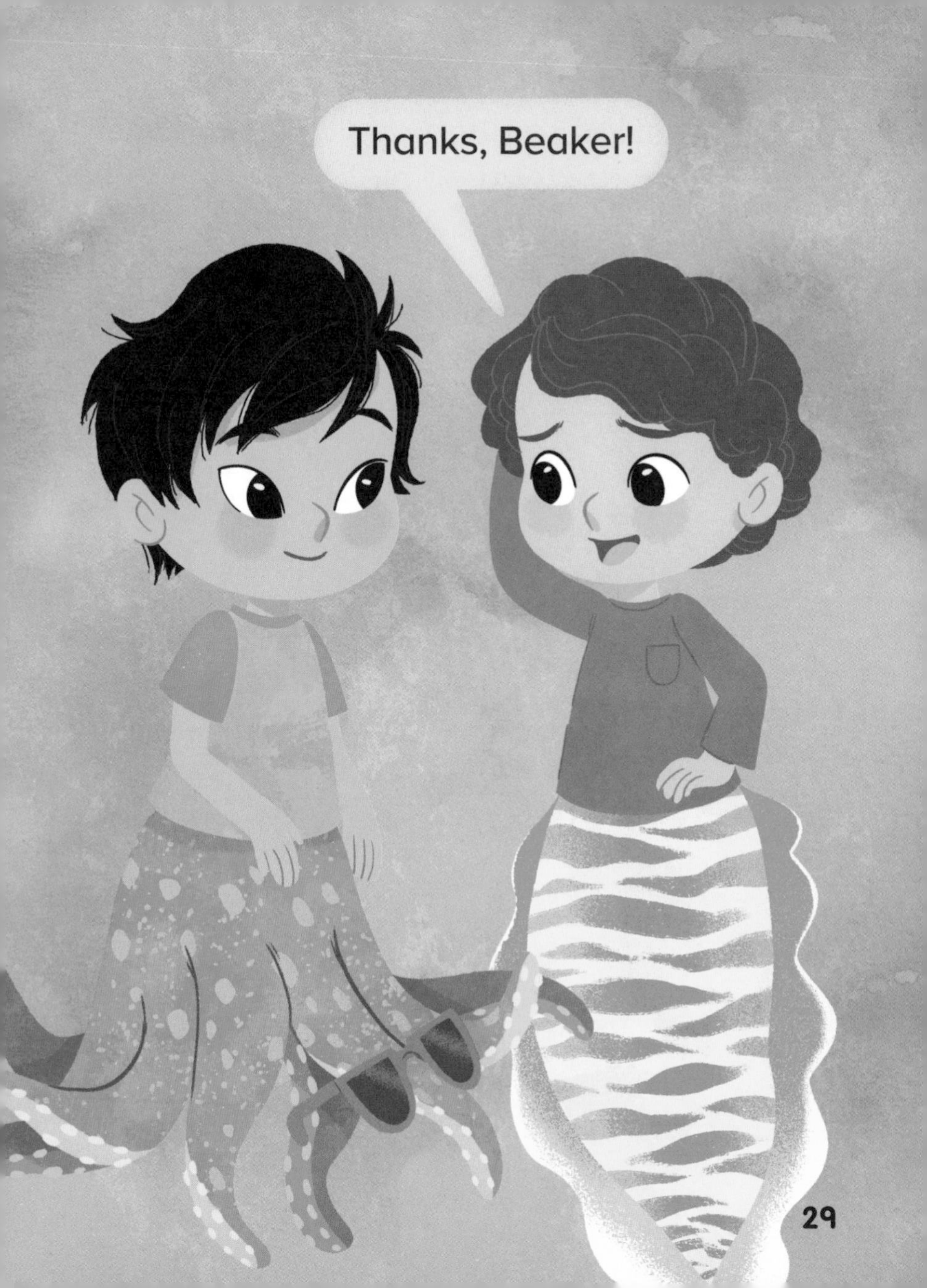
Thanks, Beaker!

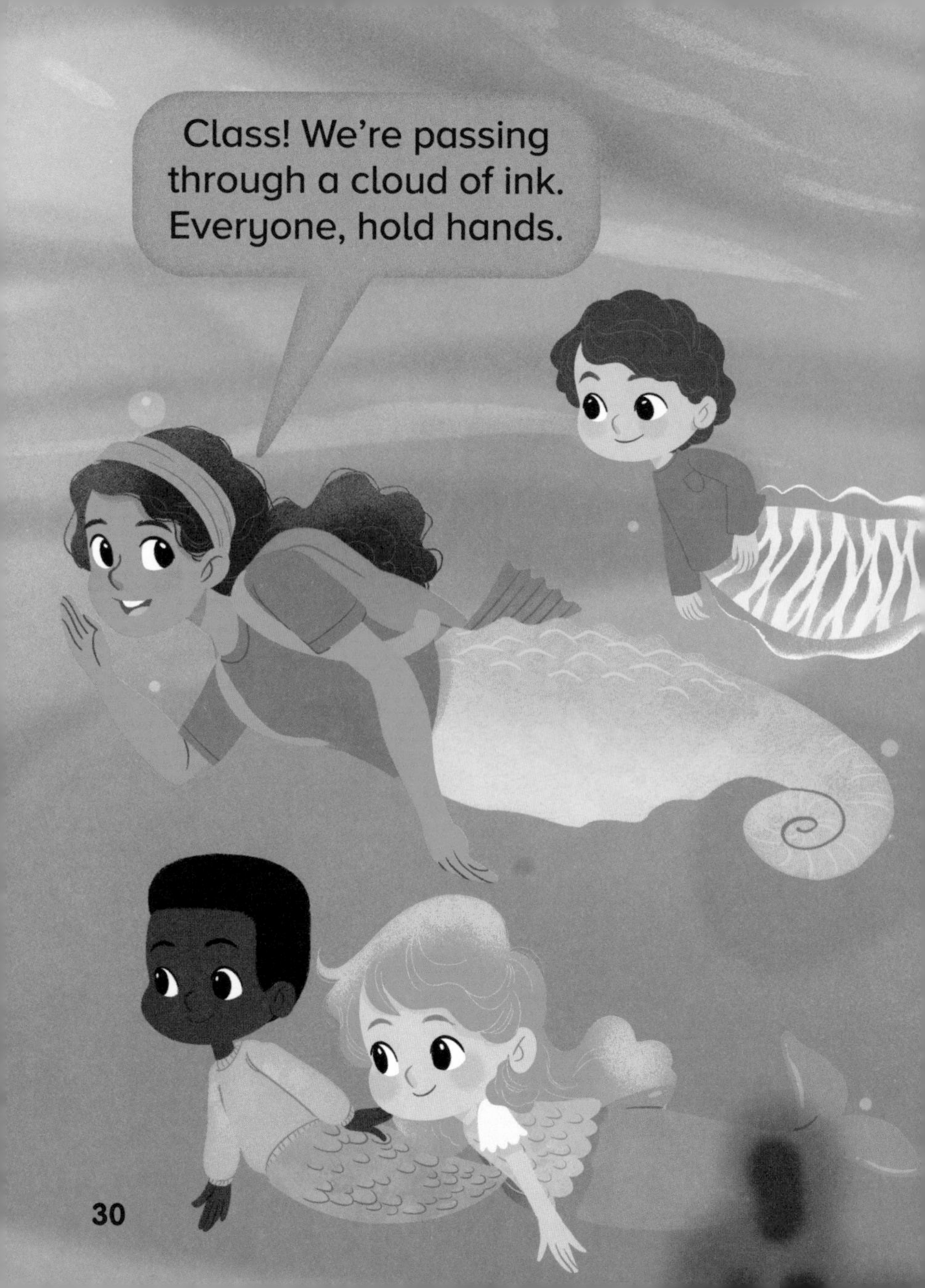
Class! We're passing through a cloud of ink. Everyone, hold hands.

Frond, where are you?
Right behind you! Can I grab your tail?
Yes. Don't get lost.

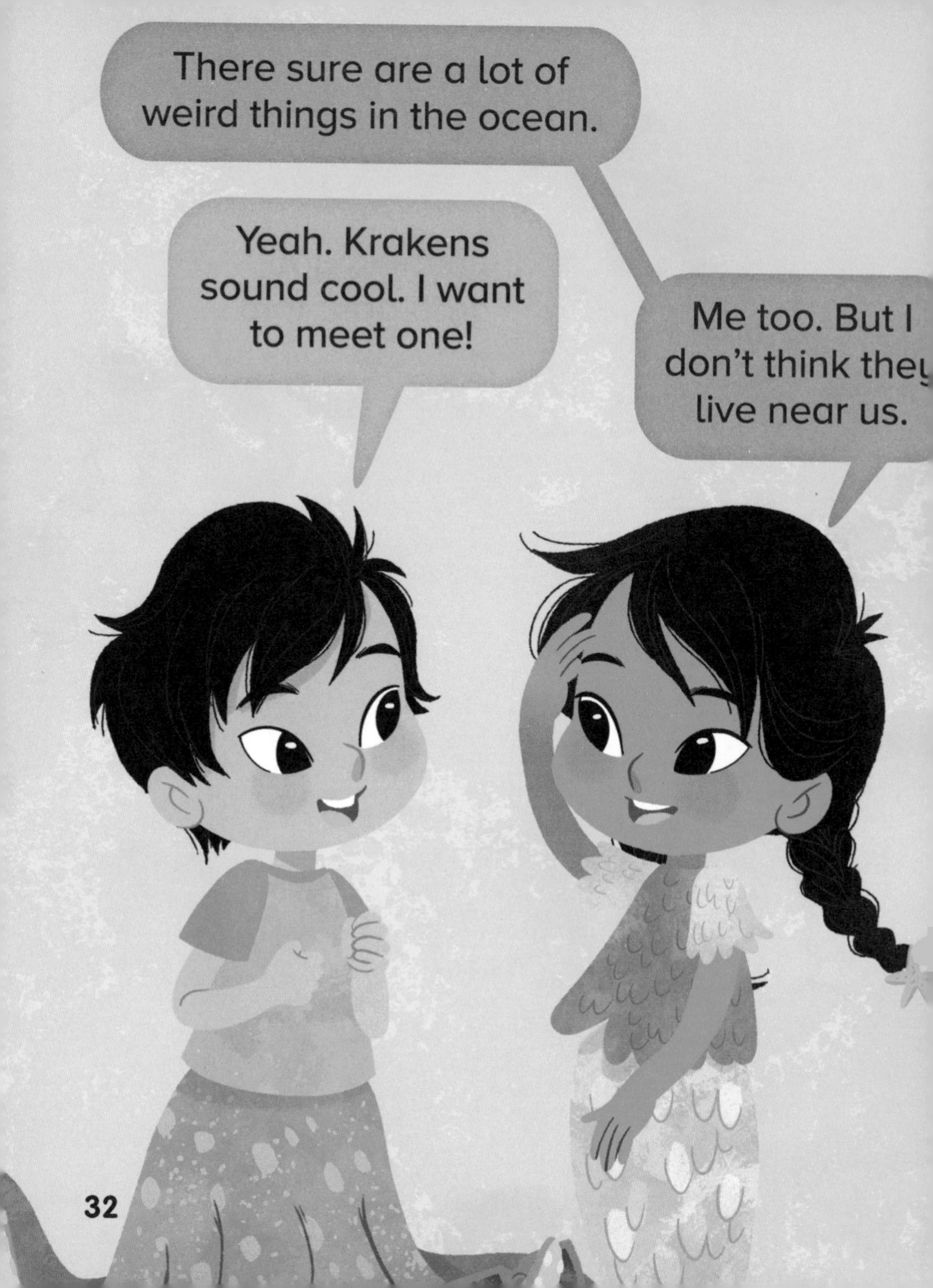
There sure are a lot of weird things in the ocean.
Yeah. Krakens sound cool. I want to meet one!
Me too. But I don't think they live near us.

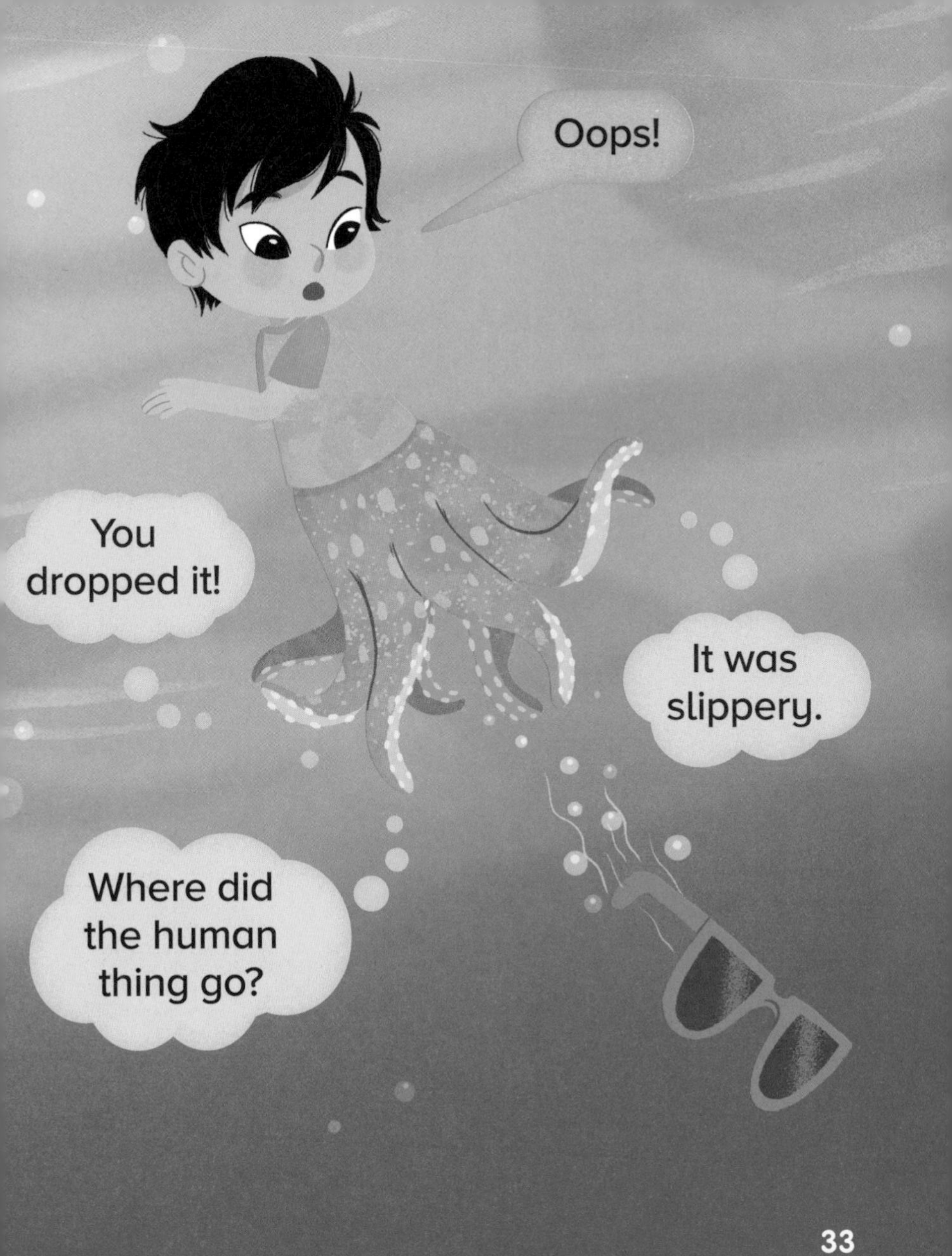
Oops!
You dropped it!
It was slippery.
Where did the human thing go?

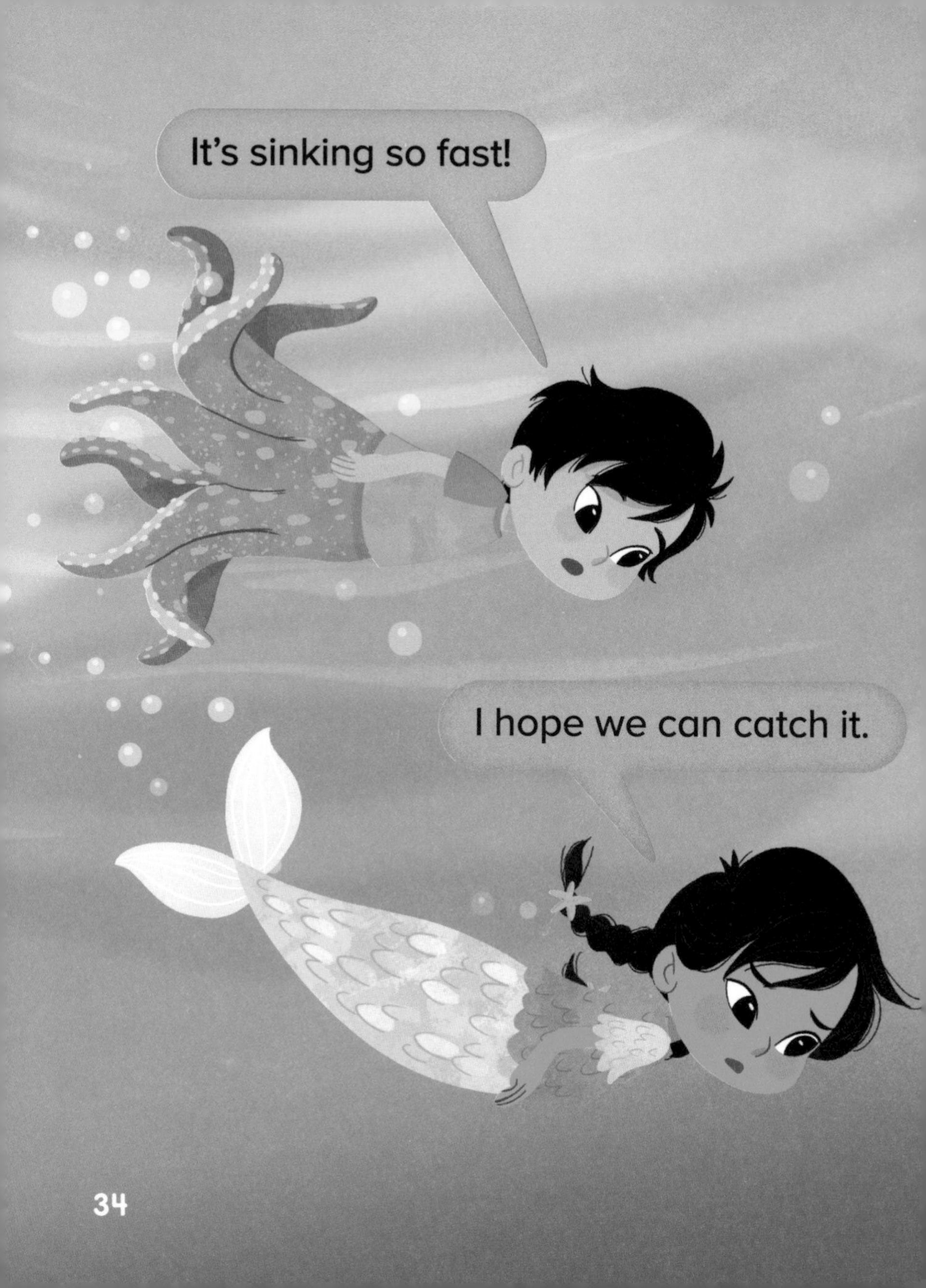
It's sinking so fast!
I hope we can catch it.

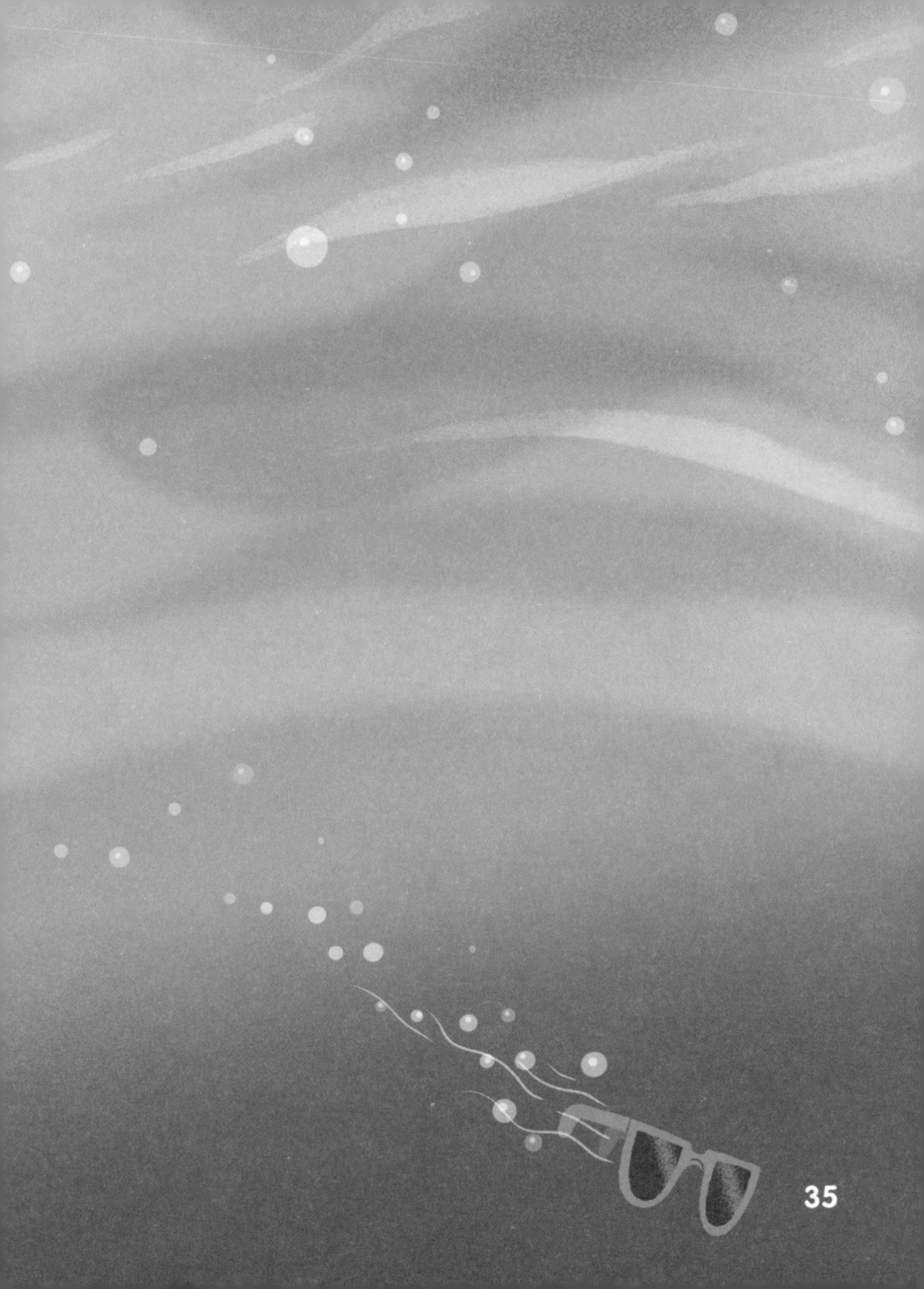

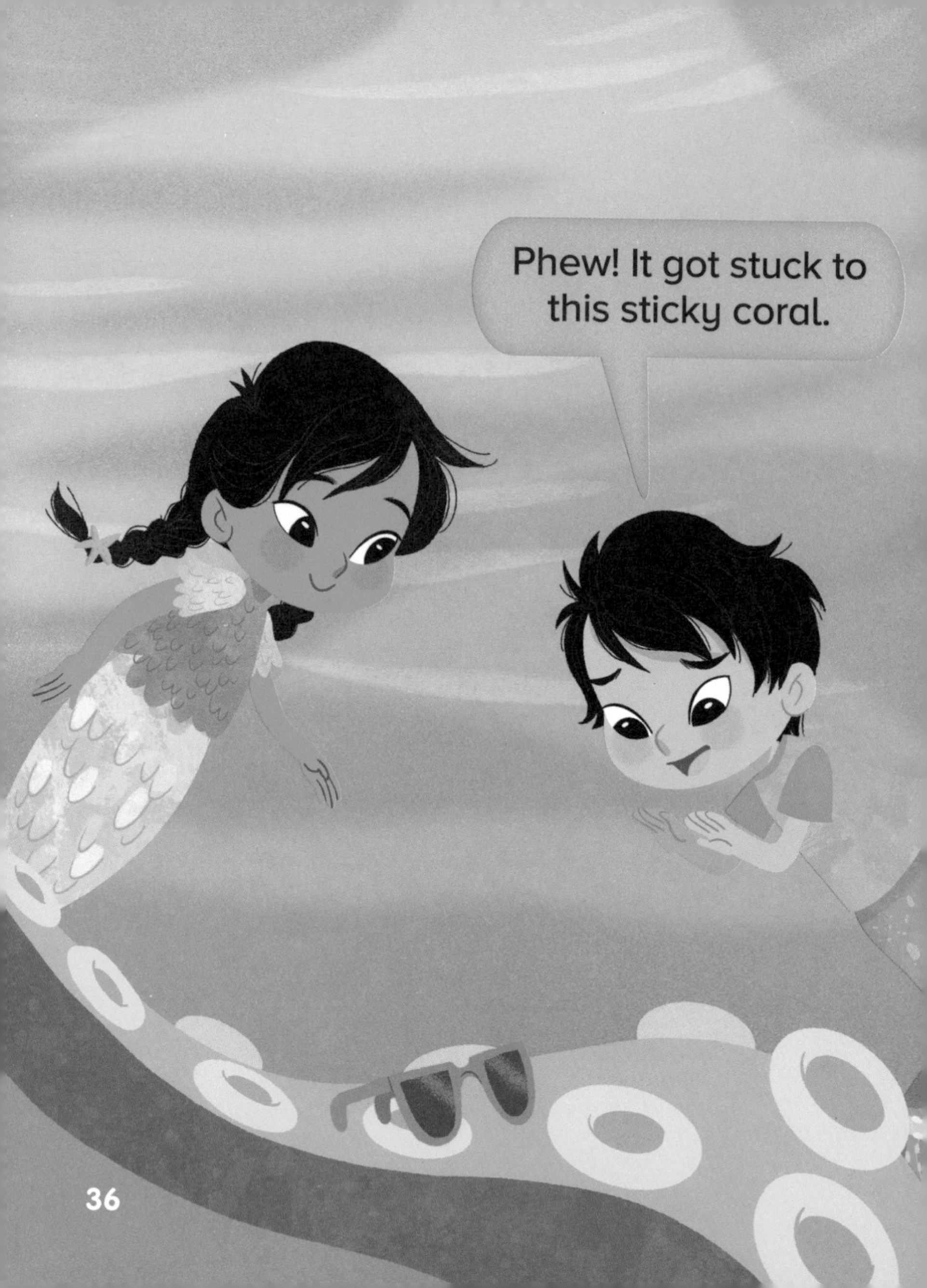
Phew! It got stuck to this sticky coral.

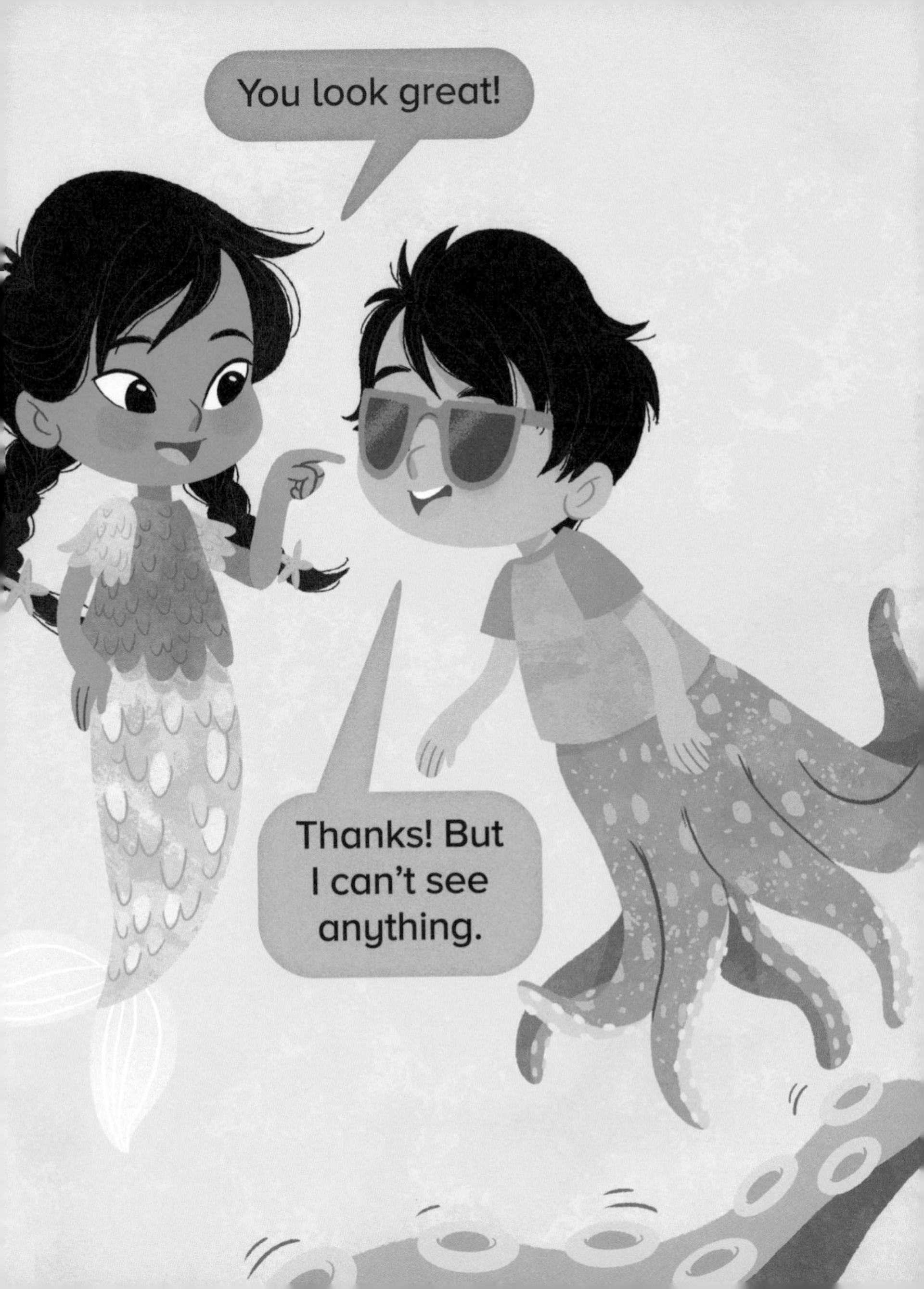
You look great!
Thanks! But I can't see anything.

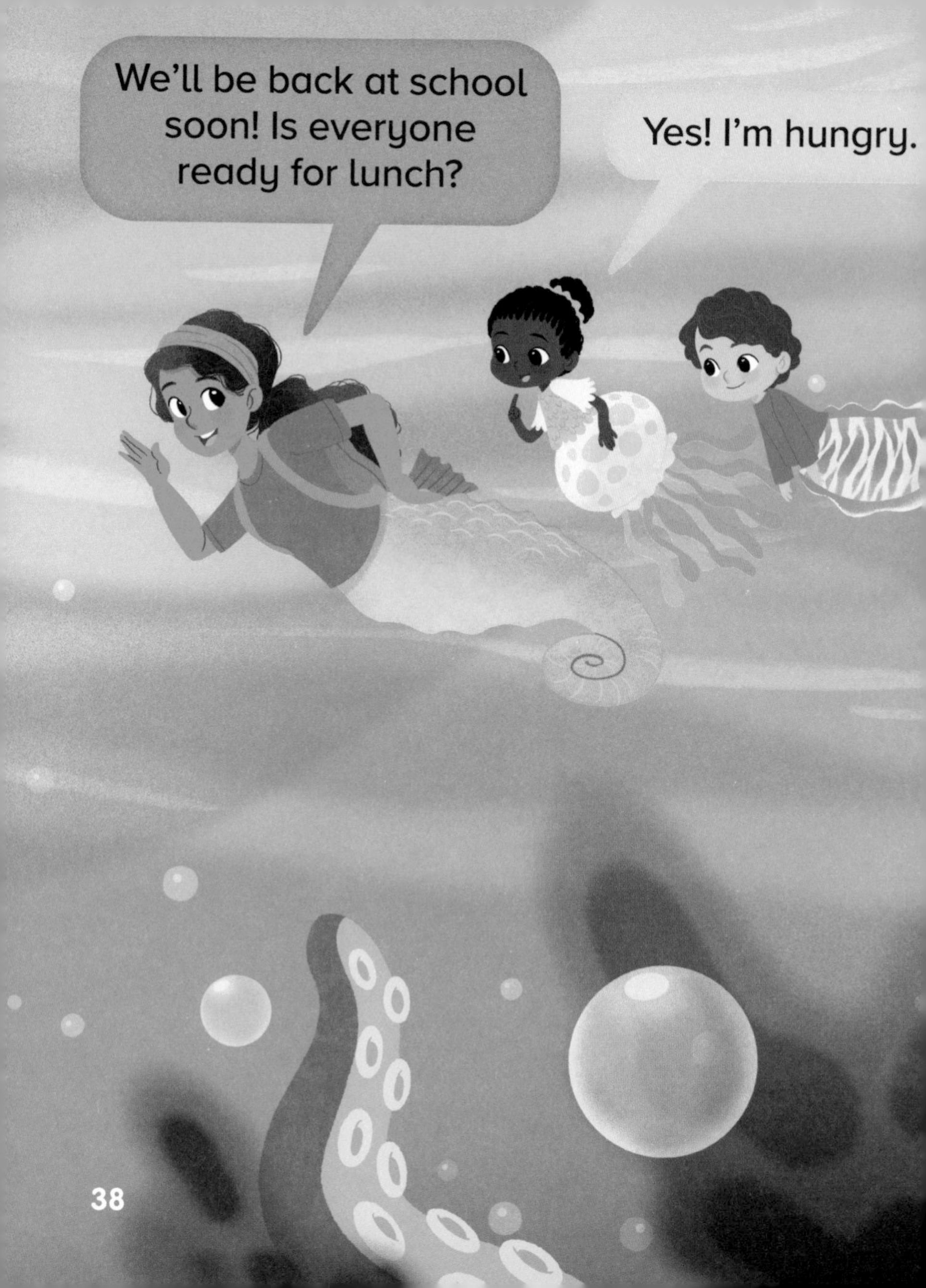
We'll be back at school soon! Is everyone ready for lunch?
Yes! I'm hungry.

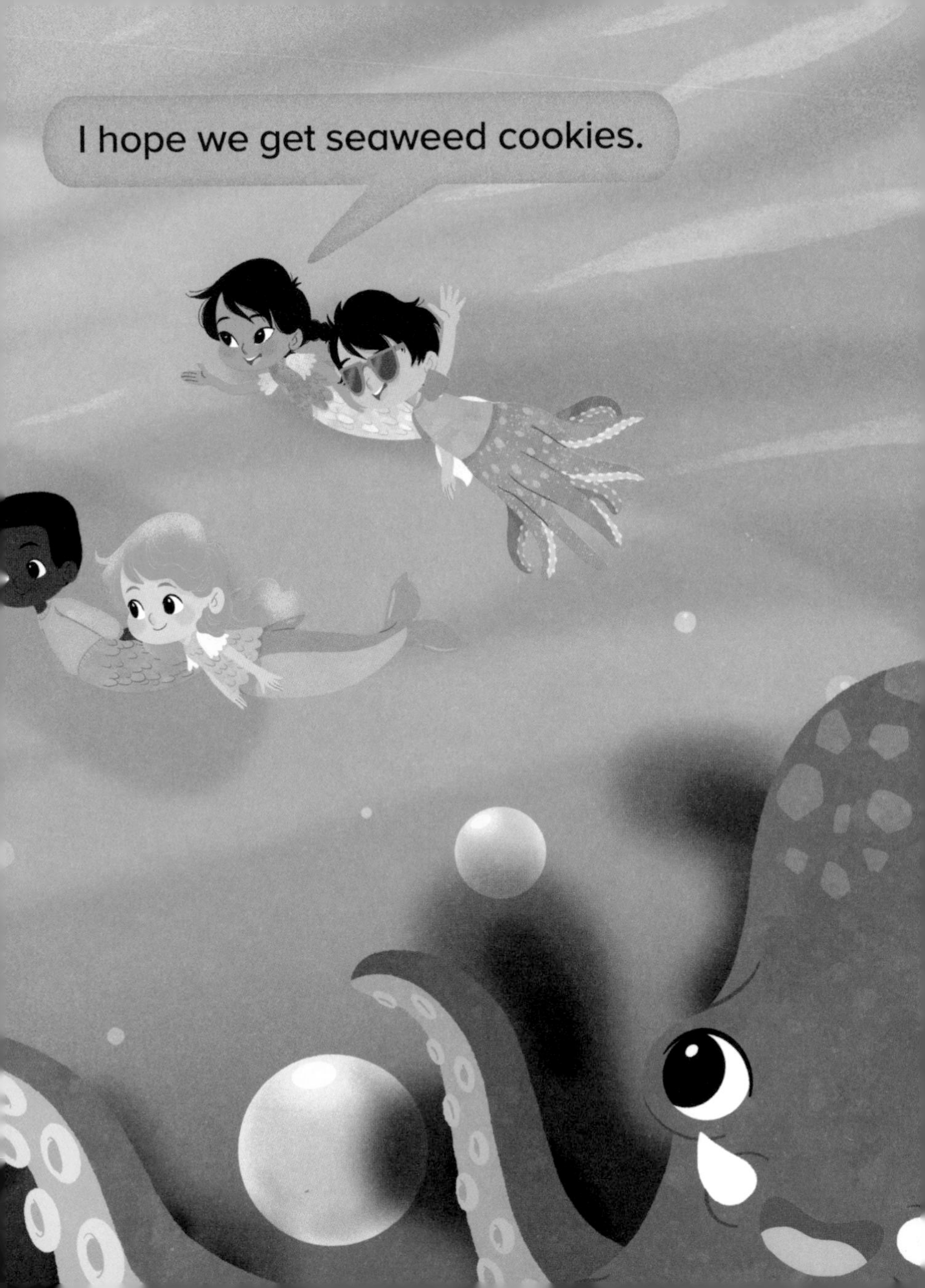
I hope we get seaweed cookies.

THE VISITOR

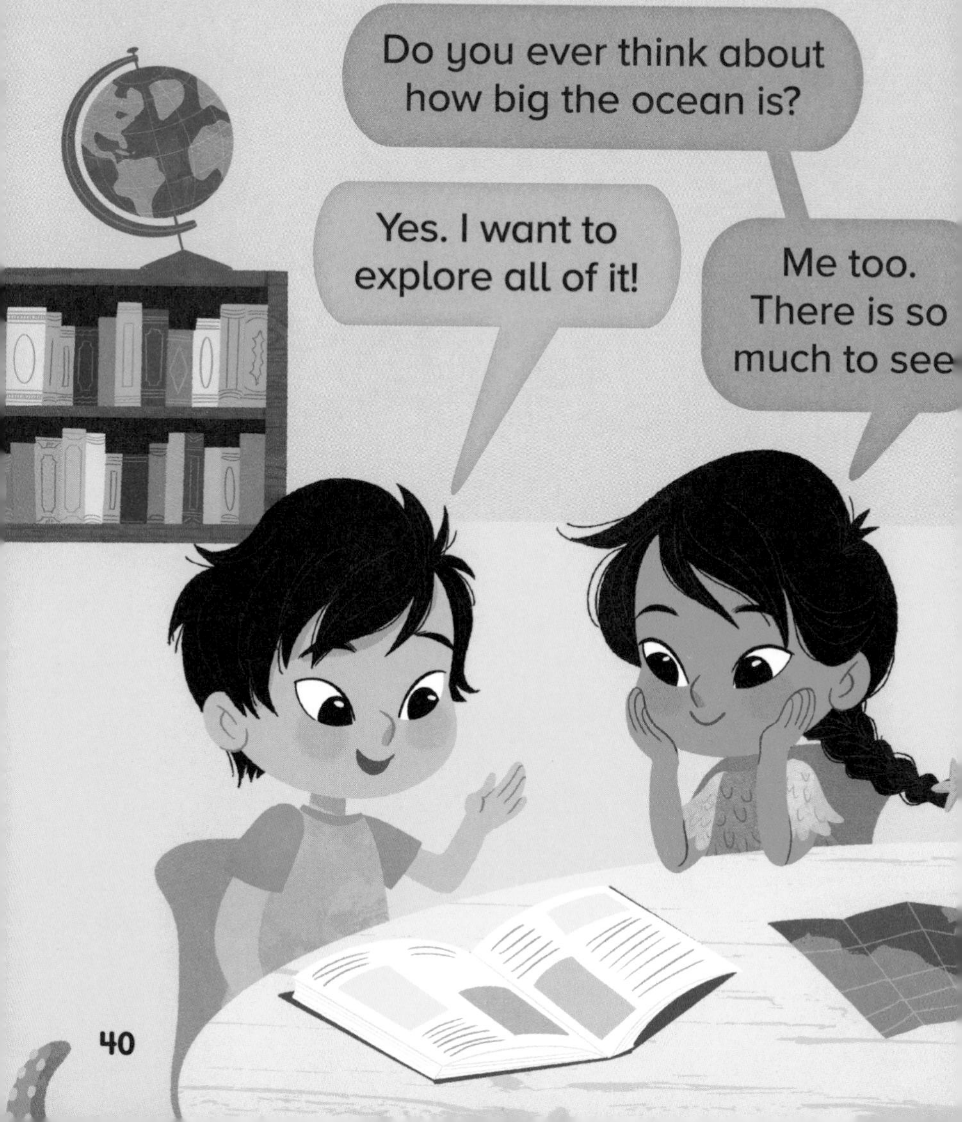
Do you ever think about how big the ocean is?
Yes. I want to explore all of it!
Me too. There is so much to see

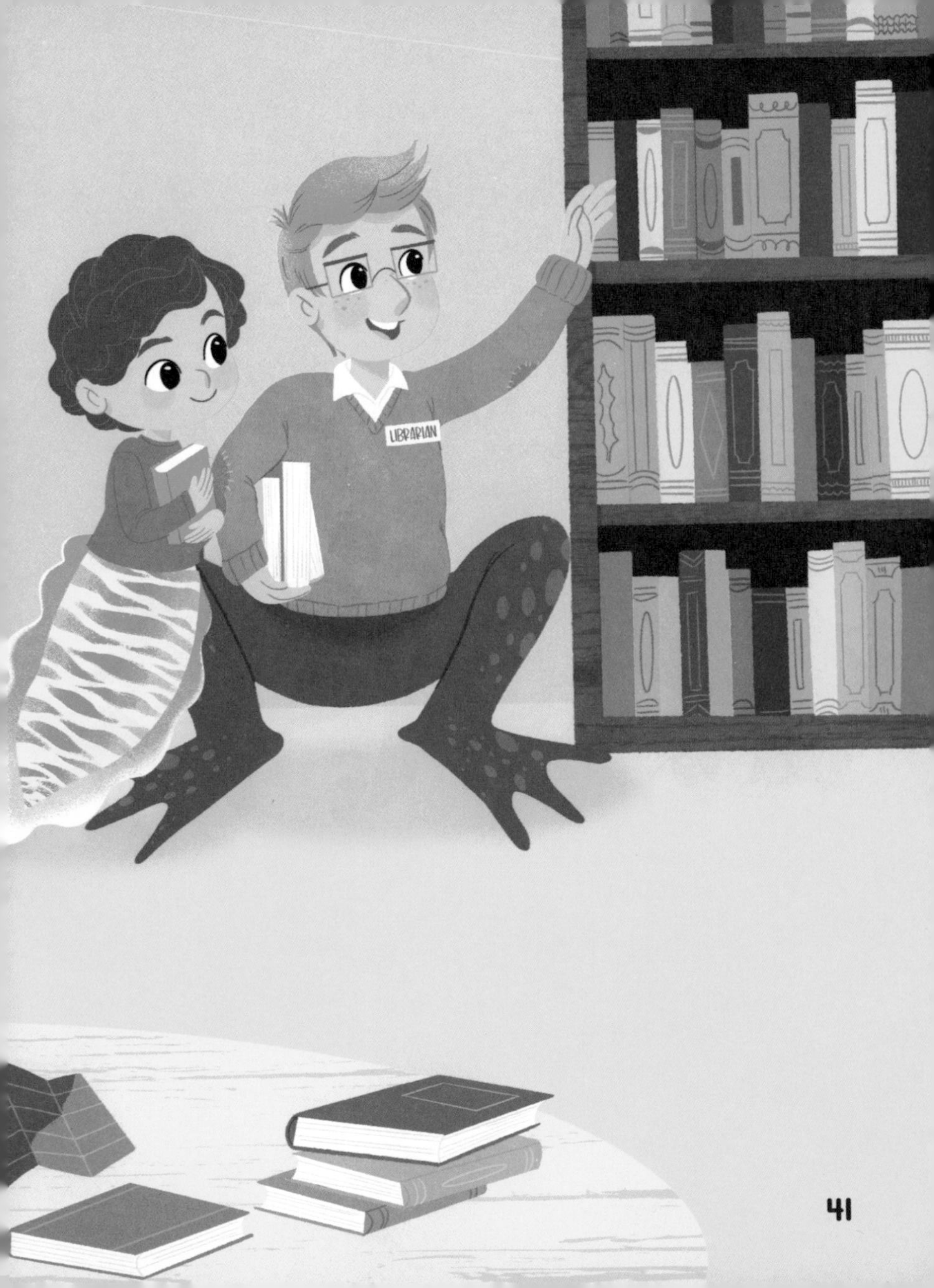
LIBRARIAN

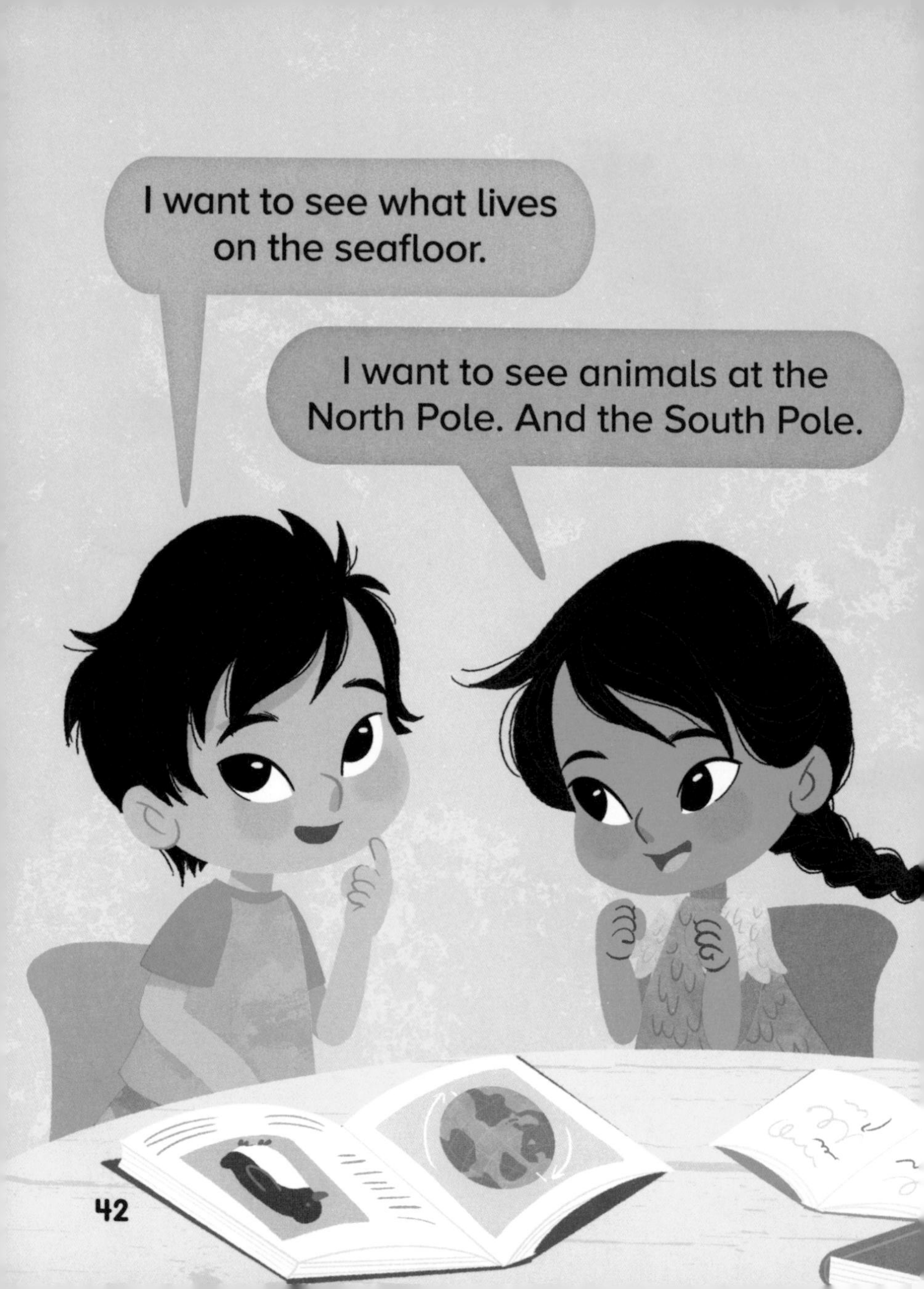
I want to see what lives on the seafloor.
I want to see animals at the North Pole. And the South Pole.

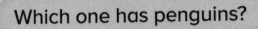

Which one has penguins?

Penguins live at the South Pole.

43

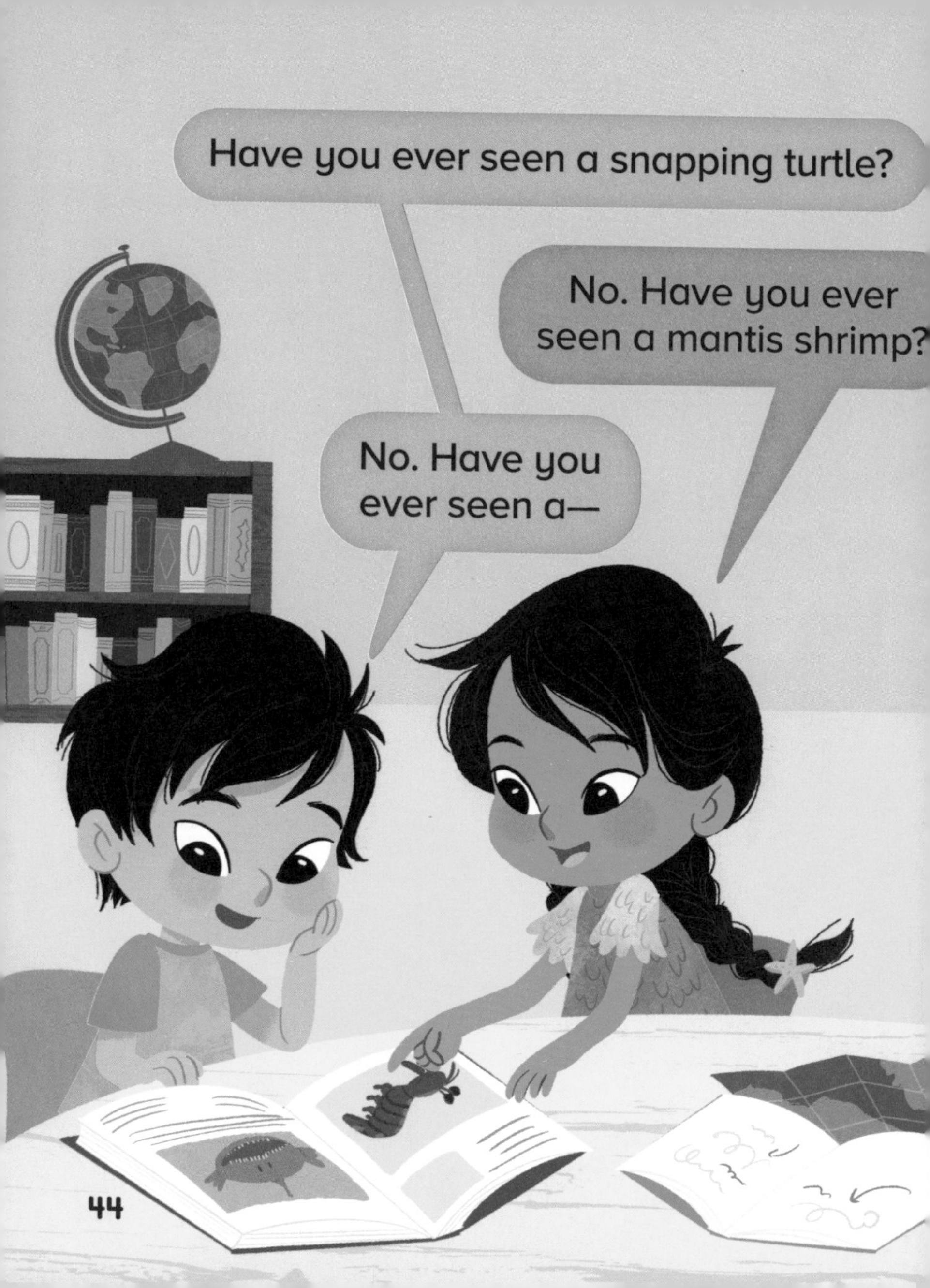
Have you ever seen a snapping turtle?
No. Have you ever seen a mantis shrimp?
No. Have you ever seen a—

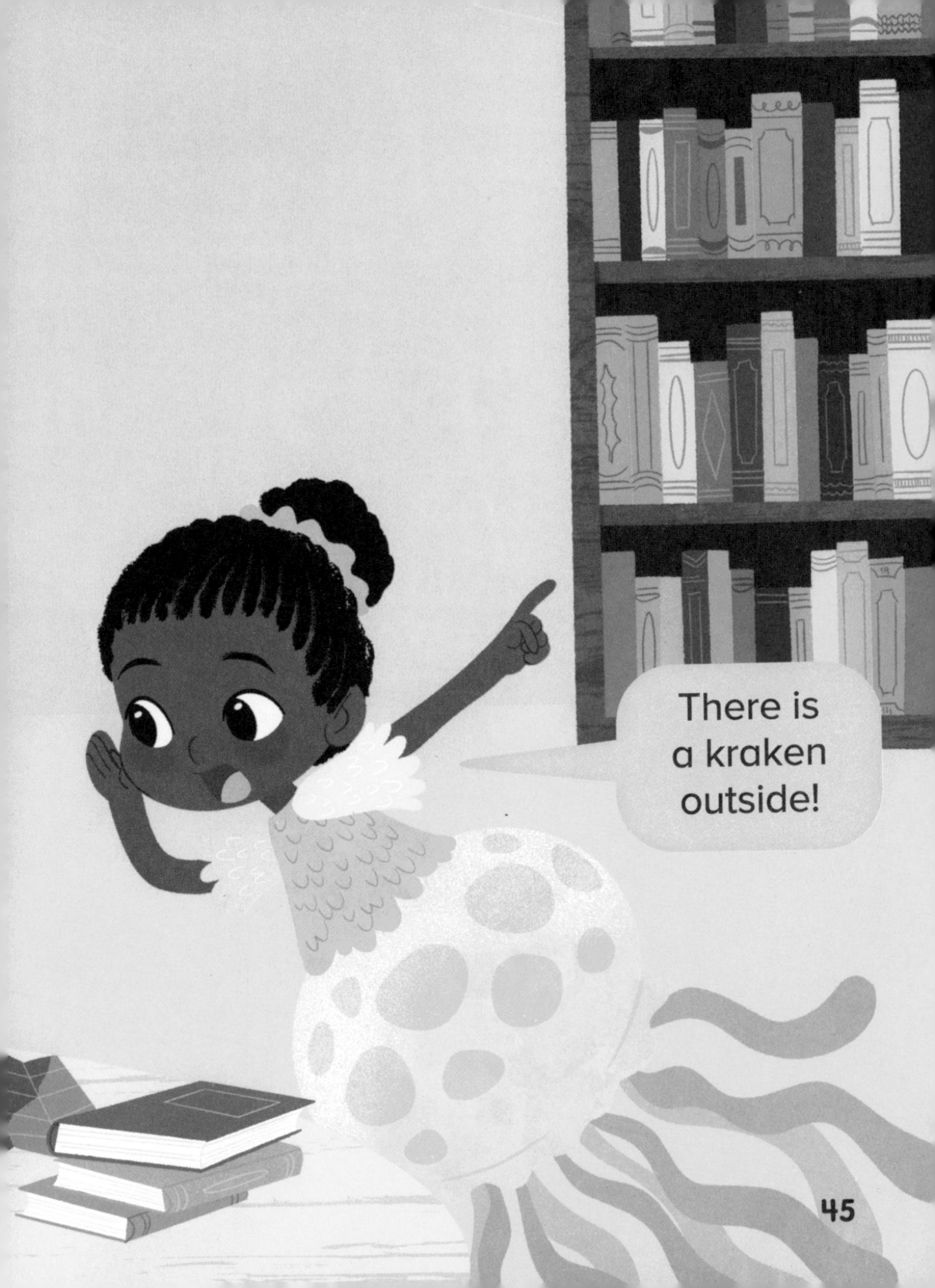
There is a kraken outside!

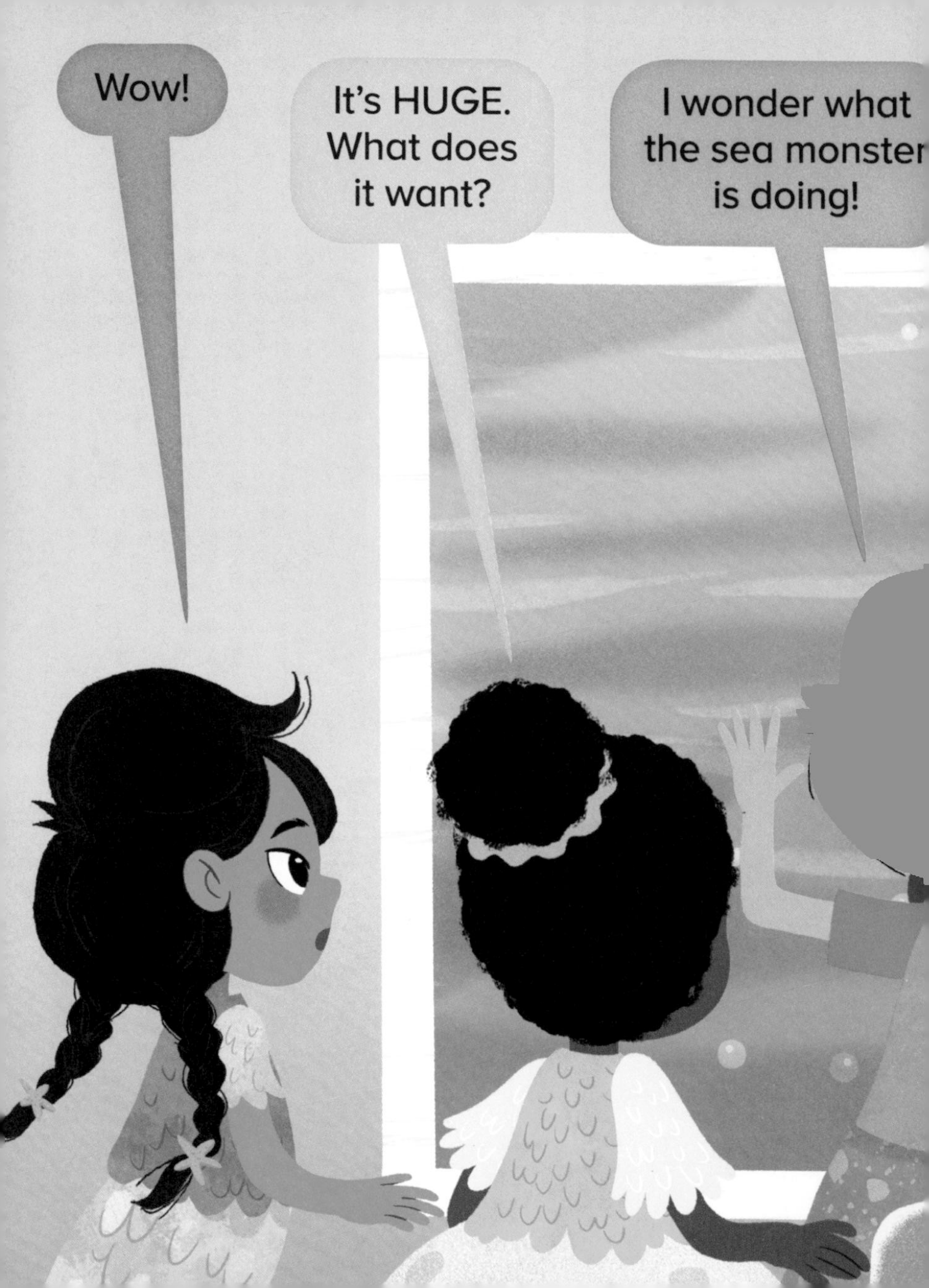
Wow!
It's HUGE. What does it want?
I wonder what the sea monster is doing!

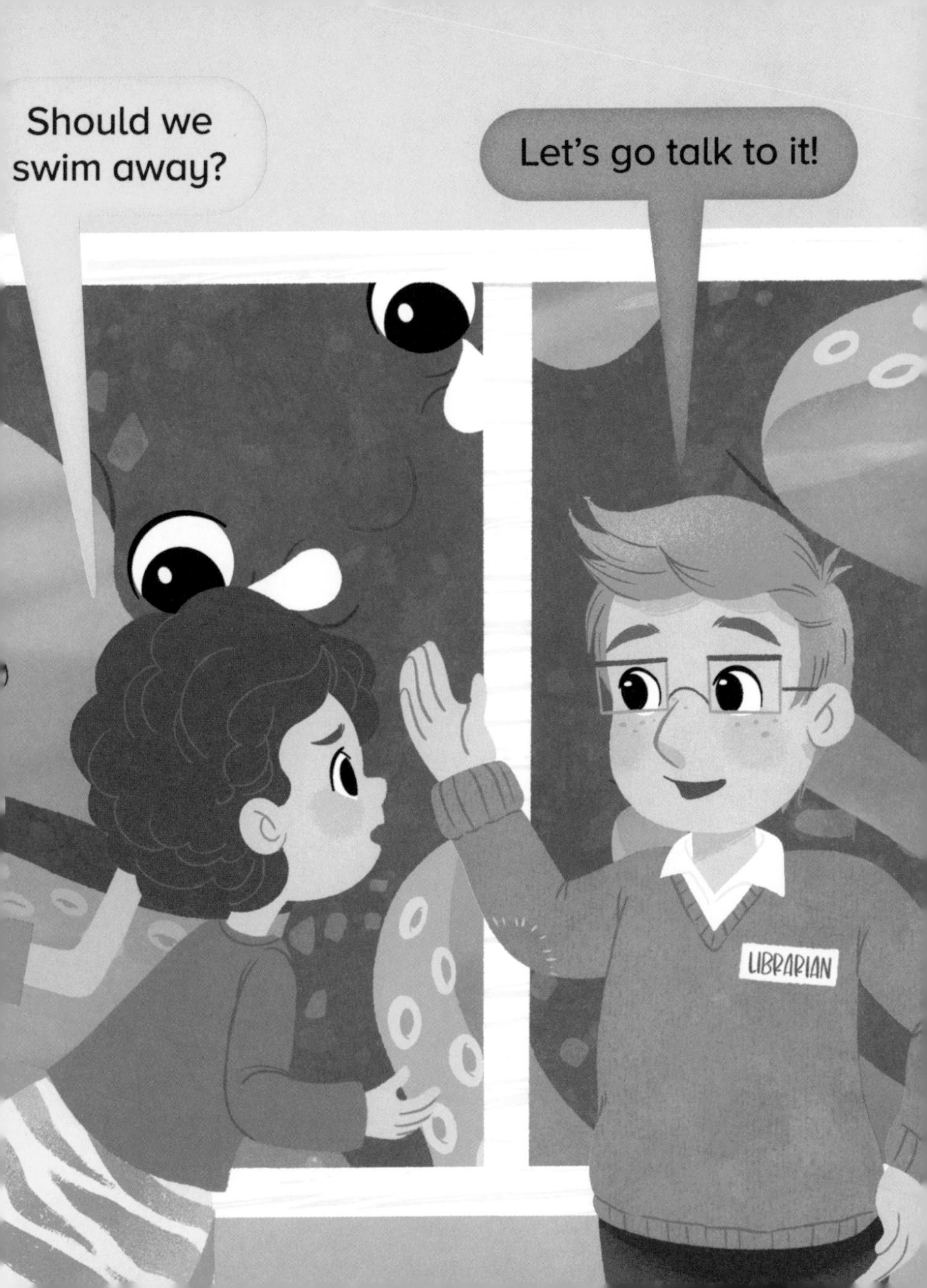
Should we swim away?
Let's go talk to it!
LIBRARIAN

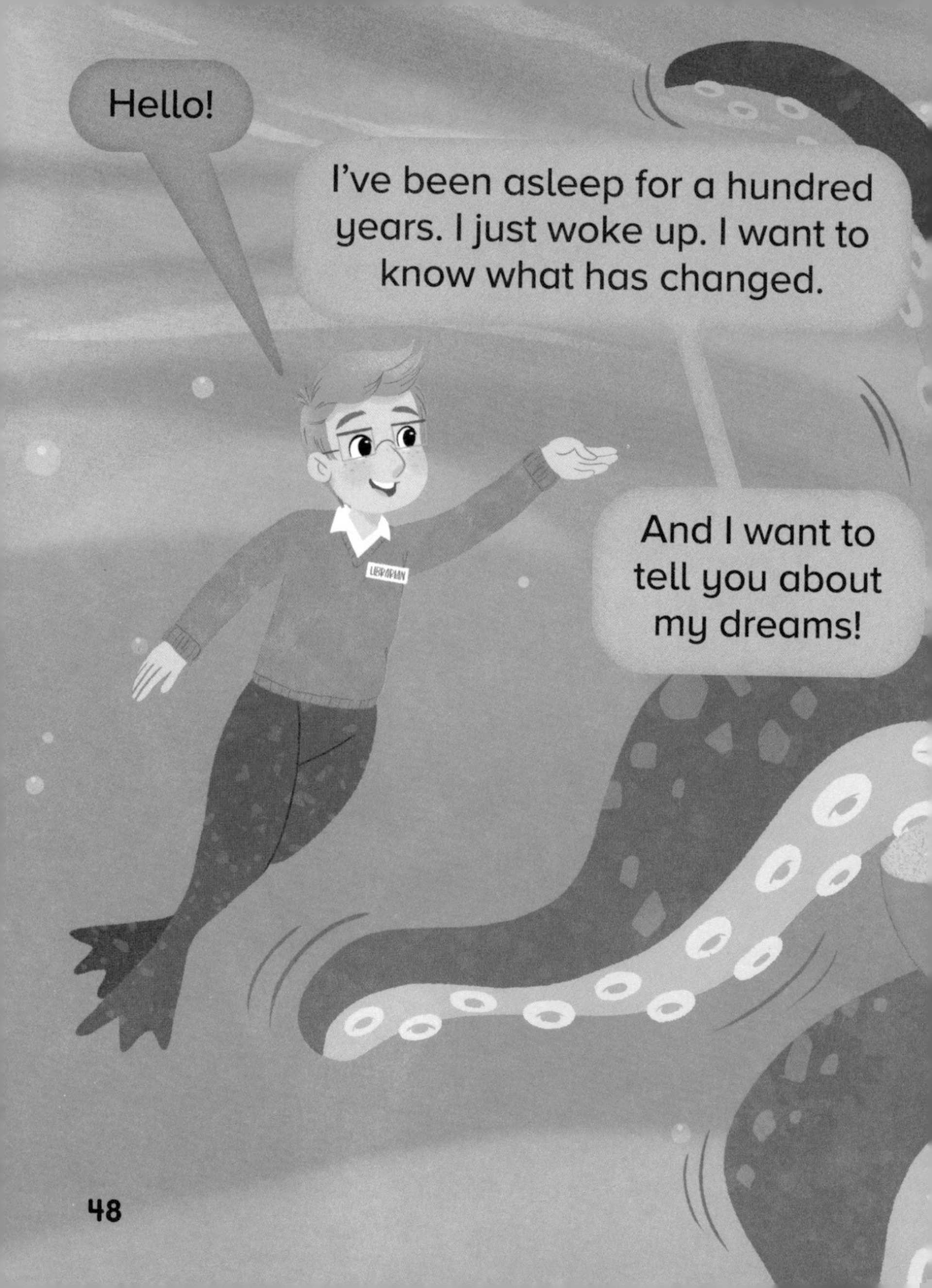
Hello!
I've been asleep for a hundred years. I just woke up. I want to know what has changed.
And I want to tell you about my dreams!
LIBRARIAN

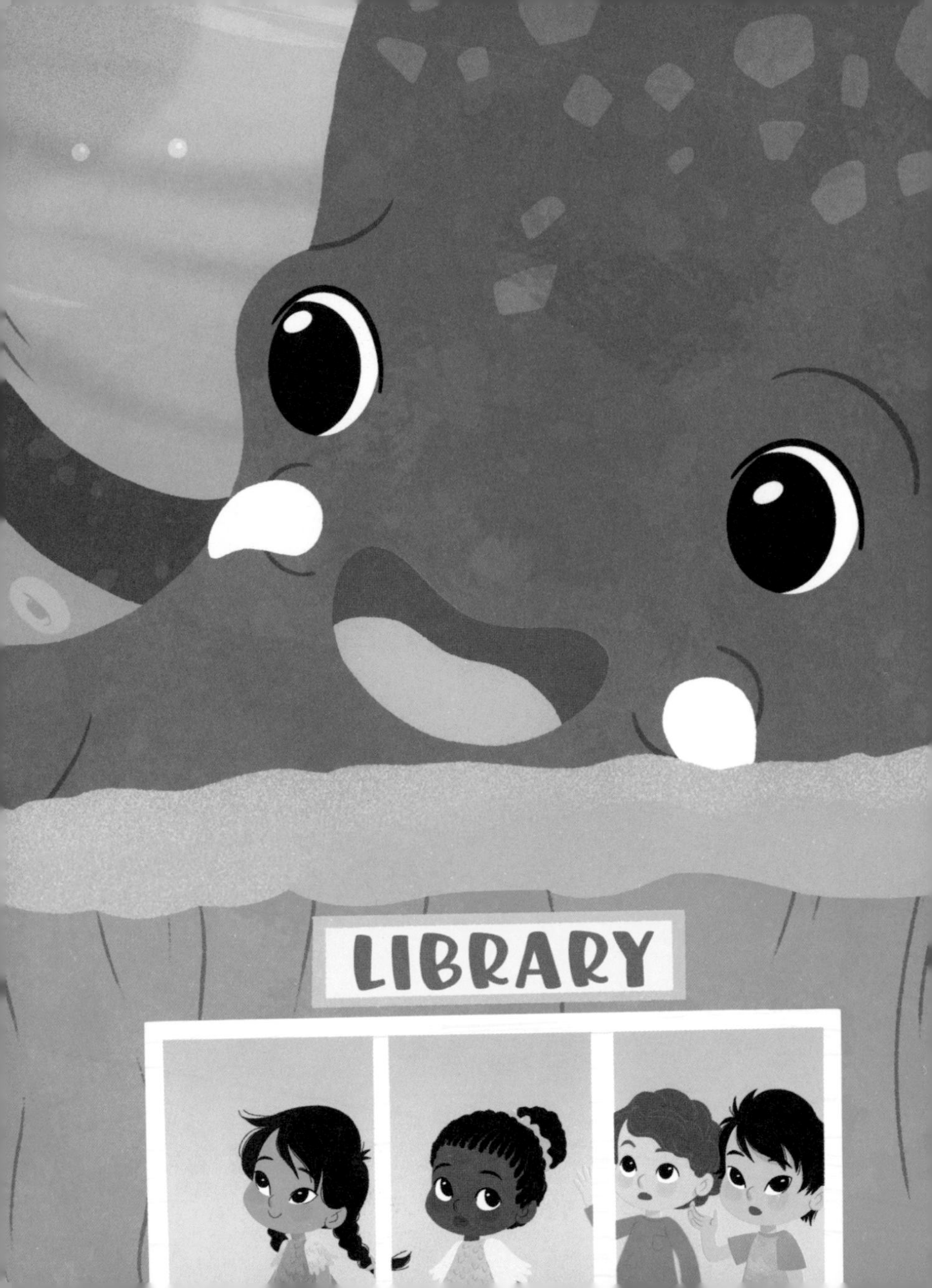
LIBRARY

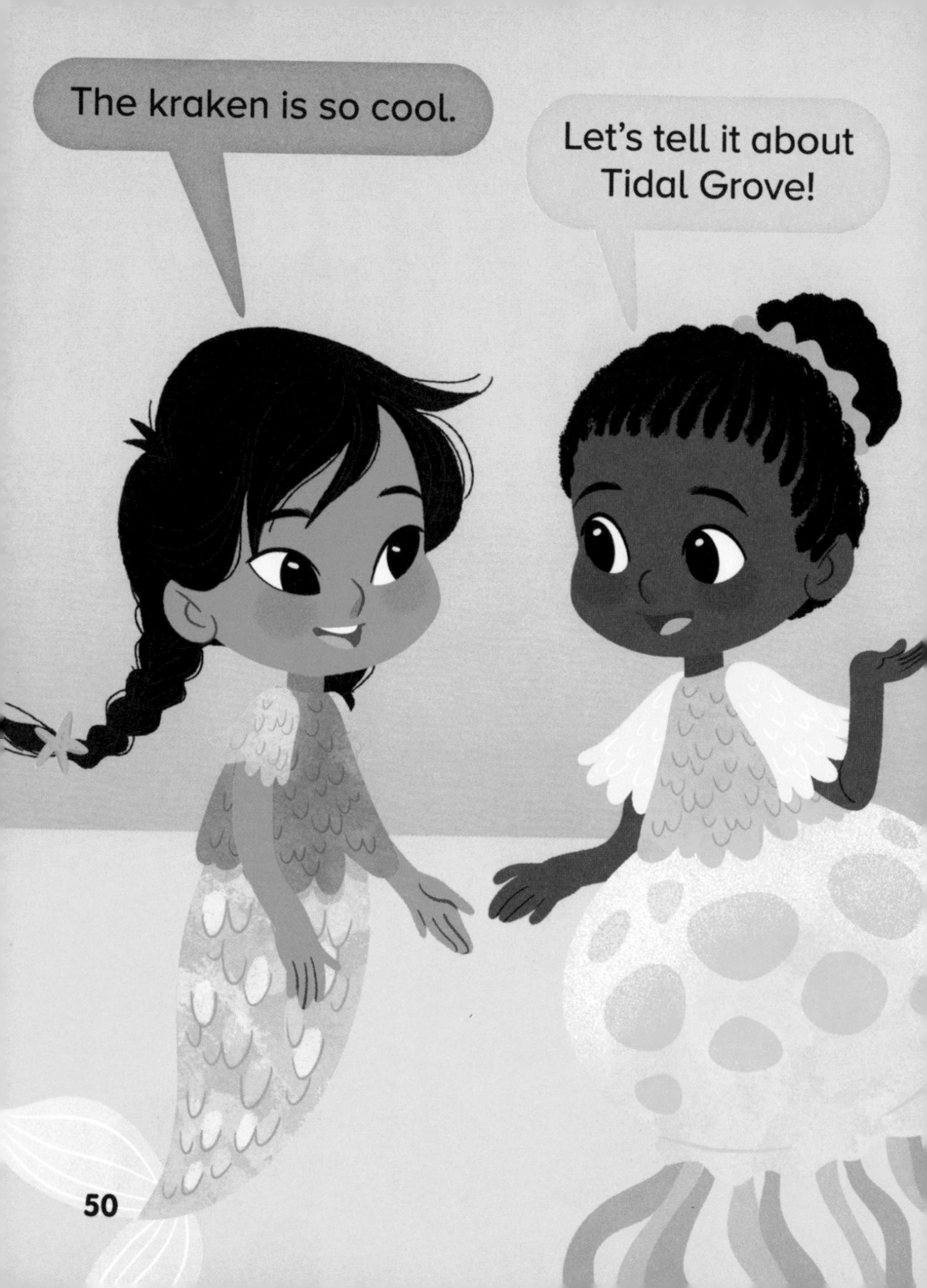
The kraken is so cool.
Let's tell it about Tidal Grove!

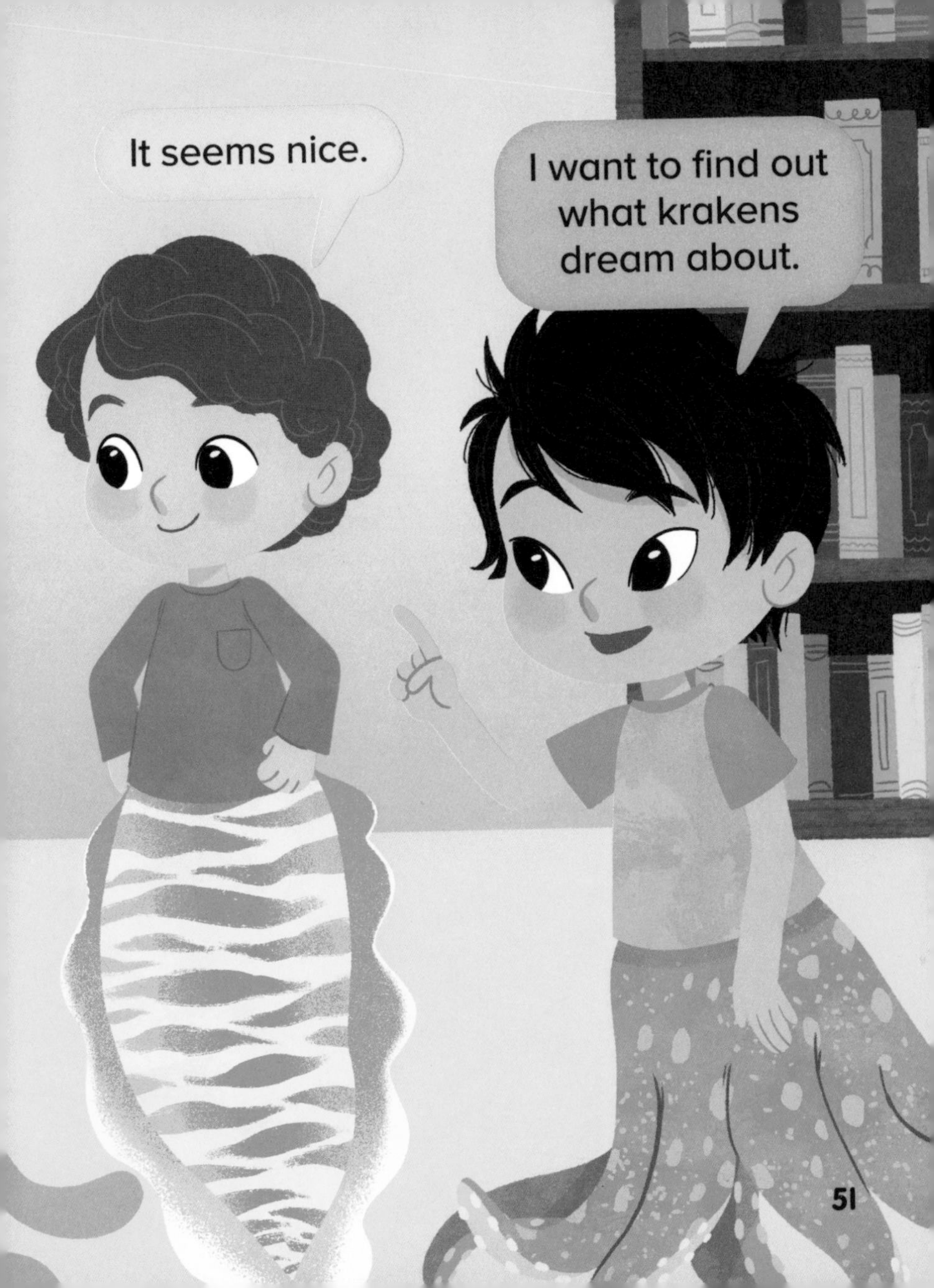
It seems nice.
I want to find out what krakens dream about.

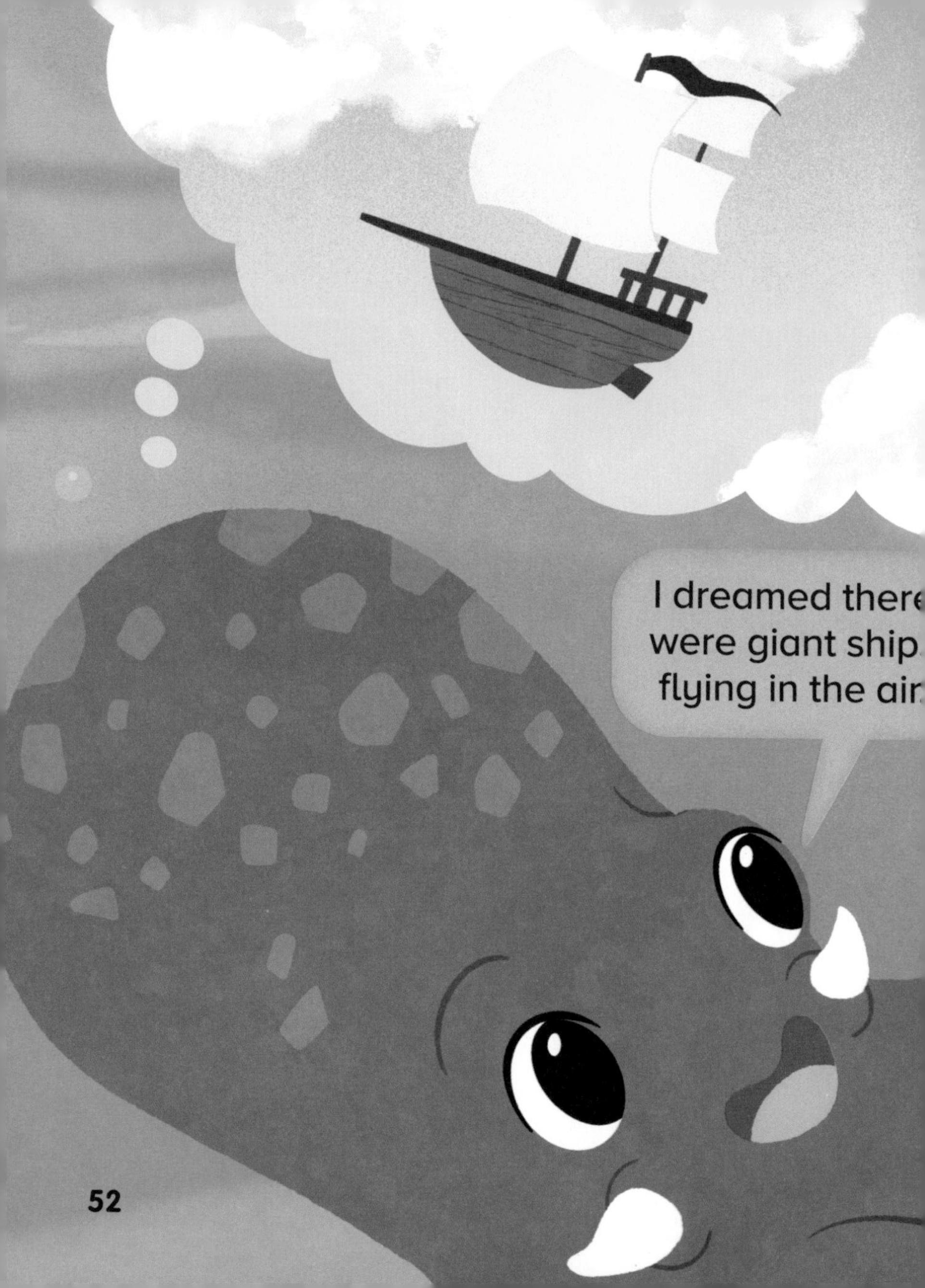
I dreamed ther
were giant ship
flying in the air

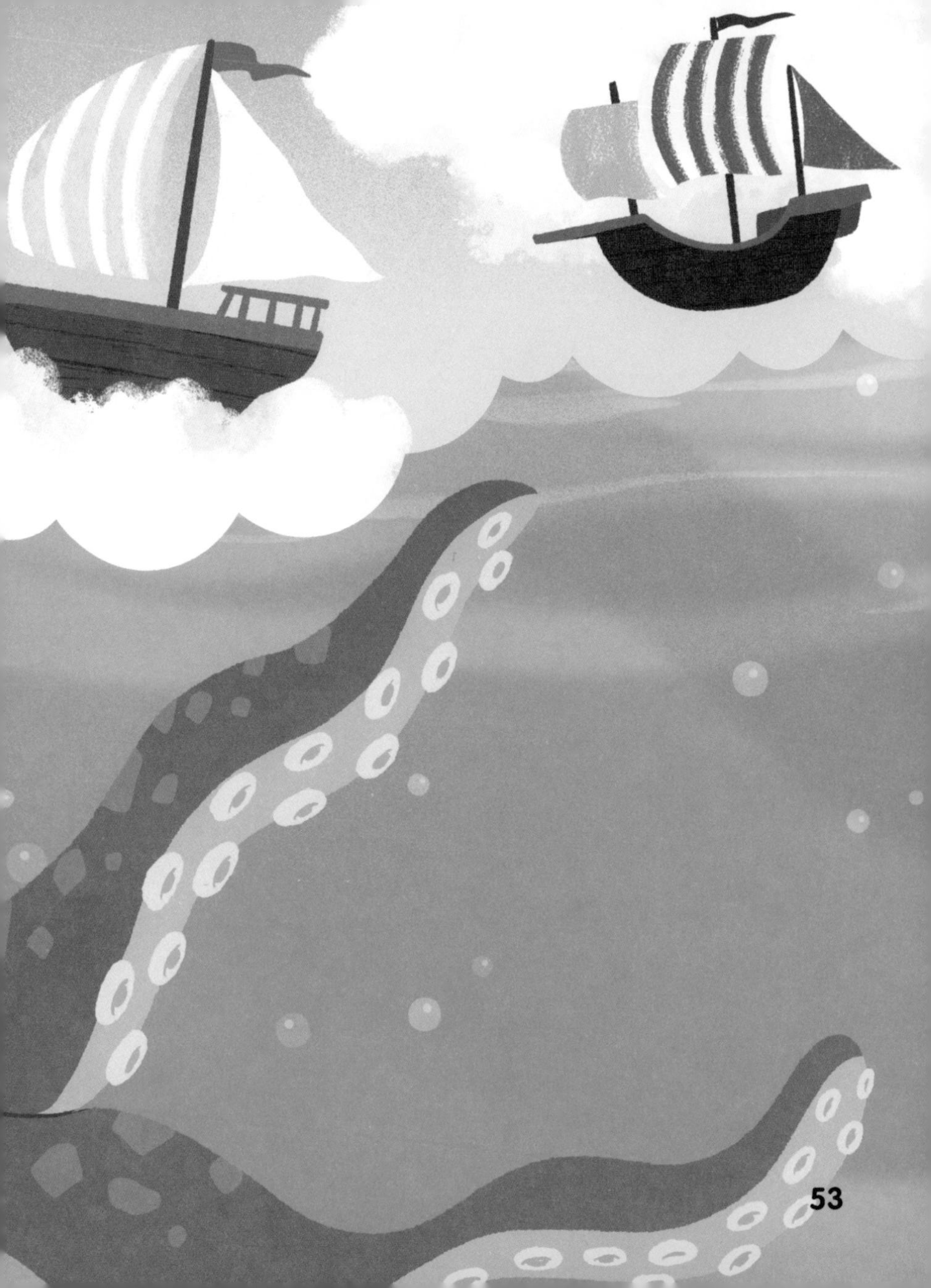

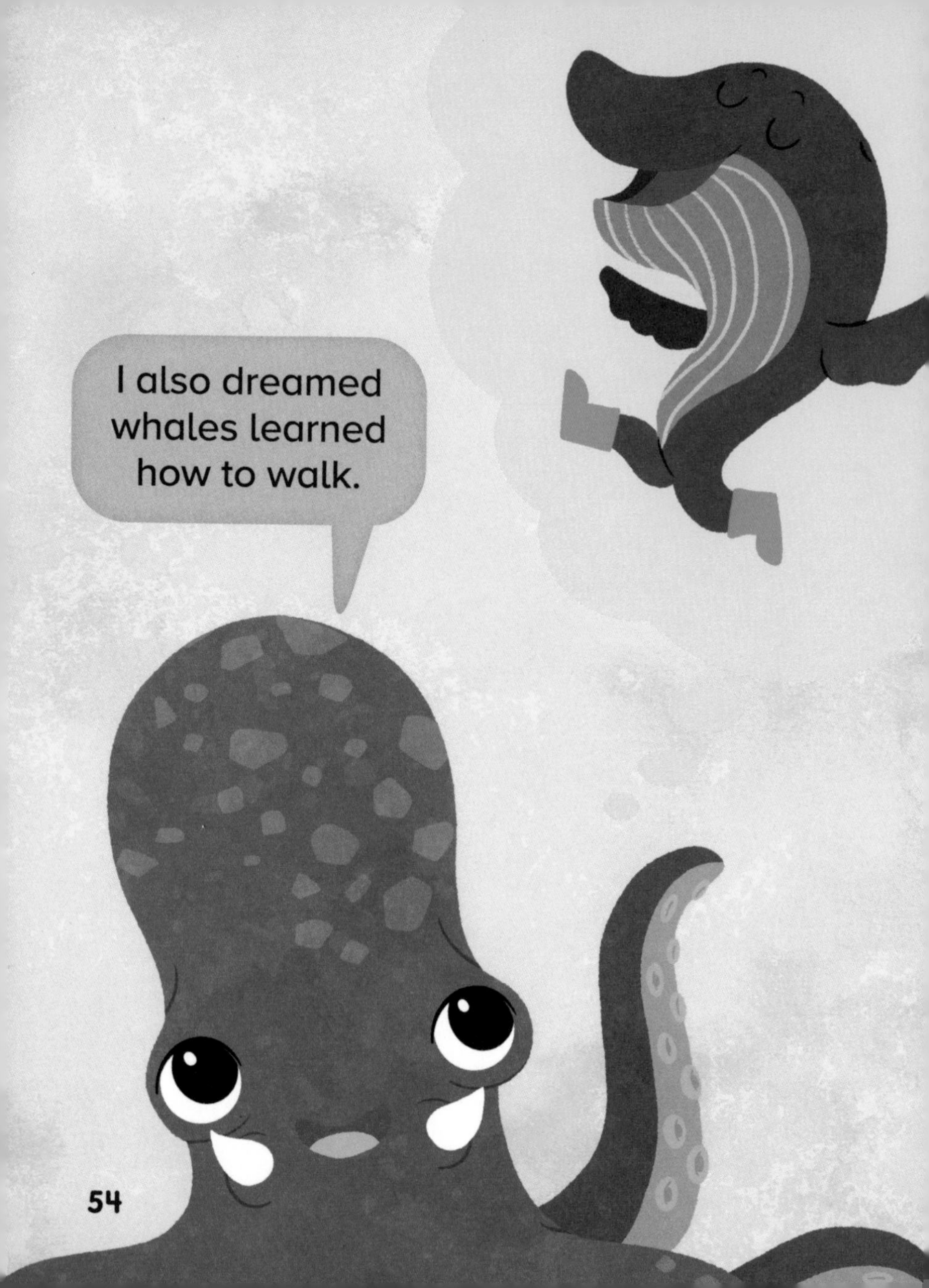
I also dreamed whales learned how to walk.

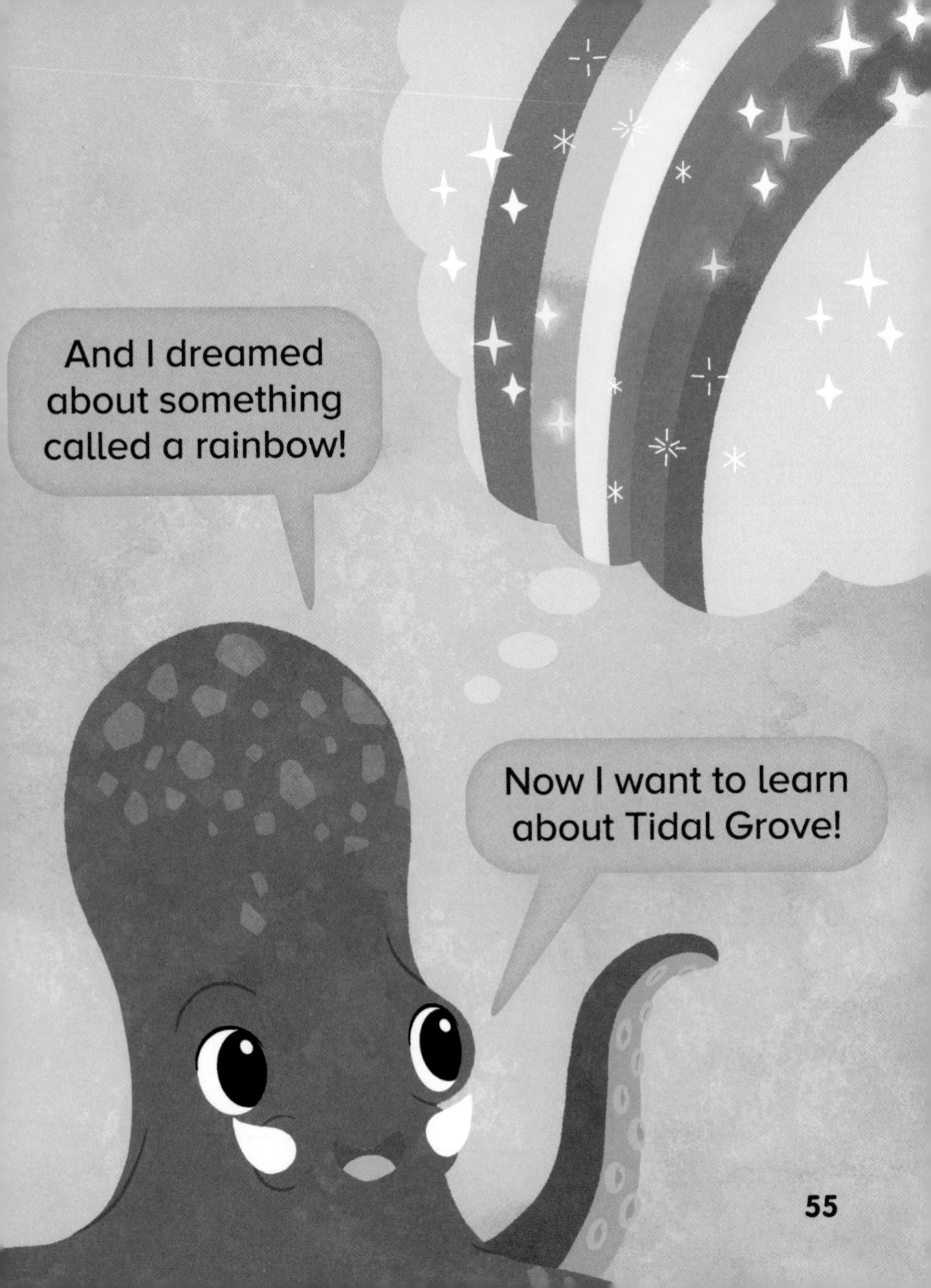
And I dreamed about something called a rainbow!
Now I want to learn about Tidal Grove!

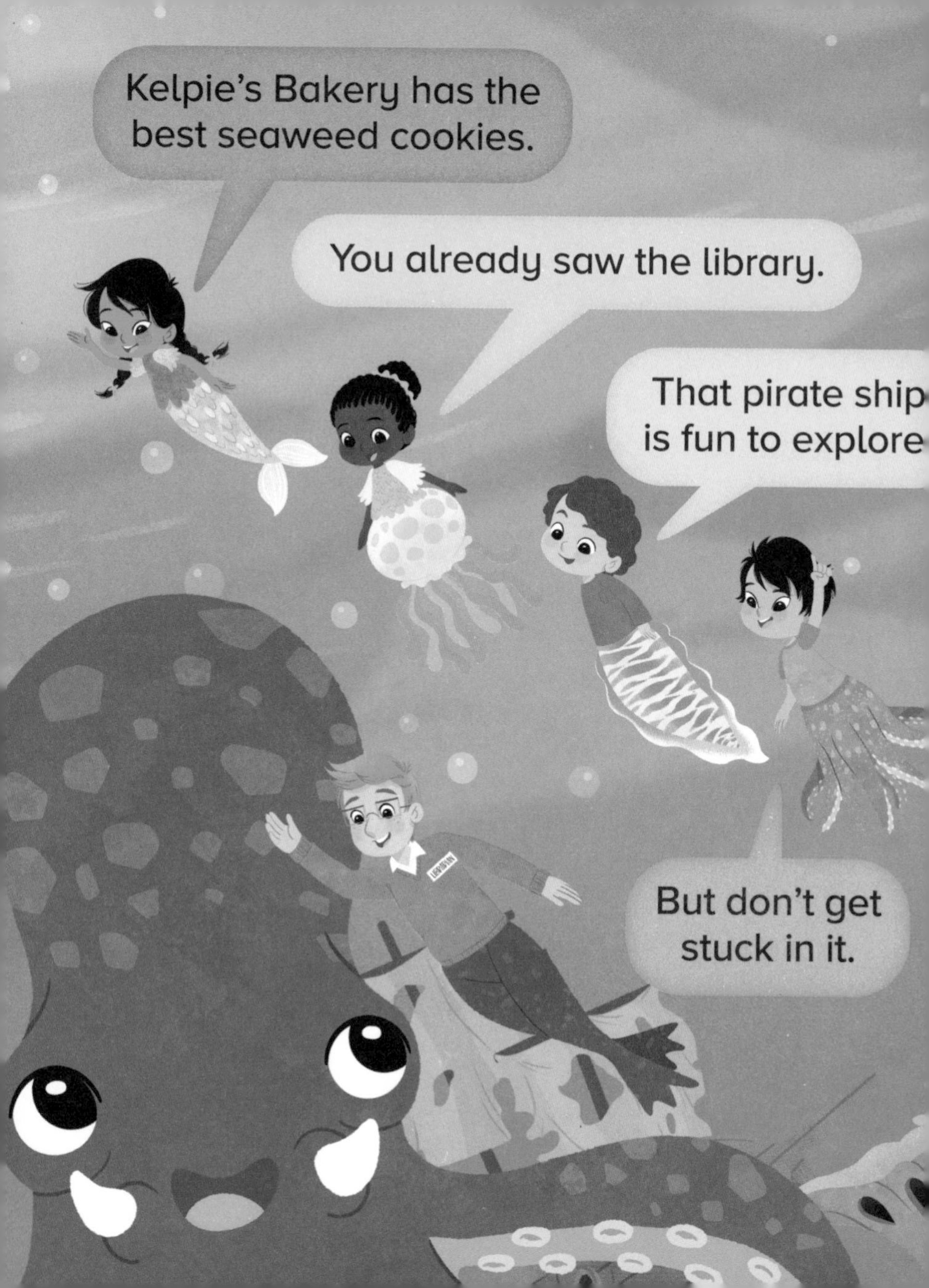
Kelpie's Bakery has the best seaweed cookies.
You already saw the library.
That pirate ship is fun to explore
But don't get stuck in it.

ABOUT THE CREATORS

KYLE LUKOFF has never met a mermaid. He would very much like to be friends with an octopus! But he would rather climb trees than go to the beach, and he would rather write books for kids than learn how to scuba dive. He is a National Book Award finalist and the Newbery and Stonewall award–winning author of lots of books, including WHEN AIDAN BECAME A BROTHER and TOO BRIGHT TO SEE.

KAT UNO was born, raised, and currently resides in Hawaii. Living on an island surrounded by the beautiful Pacific Ocean has always provided much inspiration. Kat has loved being creative ever since she was little. She enjoys illustrating children's books, and mermaids are one of her favorite subjects to draw! She is also a proud mom of two voracious readers.

YOU CAN DRAW A KRAKEN

1 Draw the outline of the head and eyes.

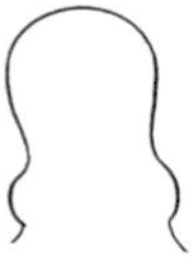

2 Draw the kraken's five tentacles.

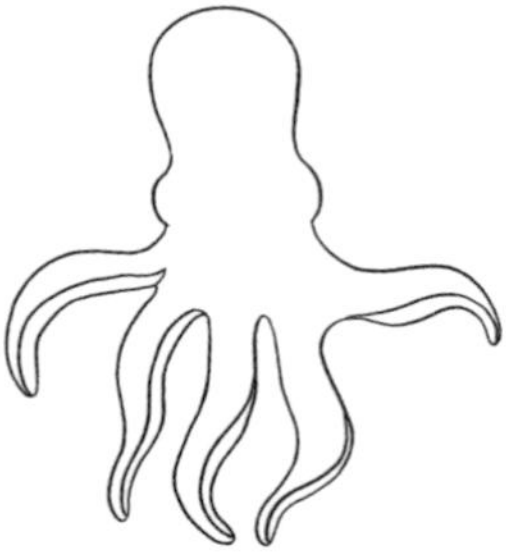

3 Add the suckers on the tentacles!

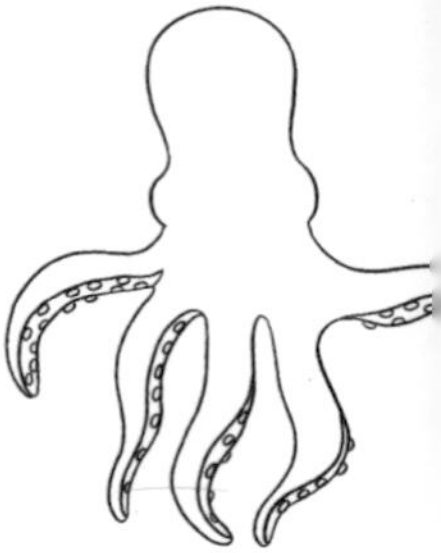

4 Draw the kraken's face! Include the eyes, tusks, and smile.

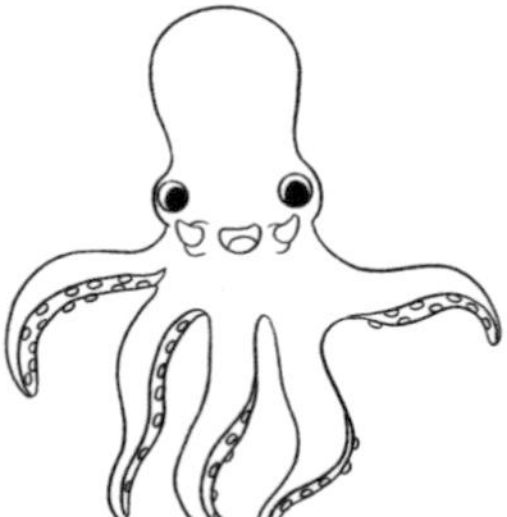

5 Decorate your kraken with a pattern.

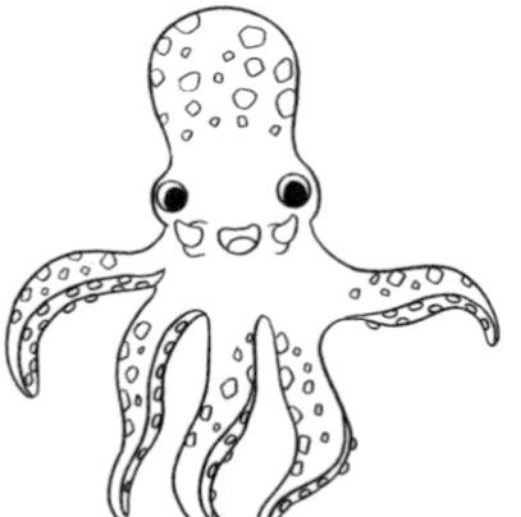

6 Color in your drawing!

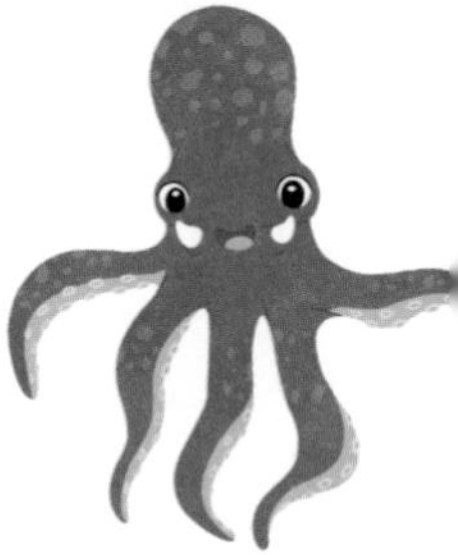

WHAT'S YOUR STORY?

Vera and Beaker meet a kraken.
Imagine that **you** meet a friendly sea monster!
What does the monster look like?
What questions would you ask it?
Write and draw your story!

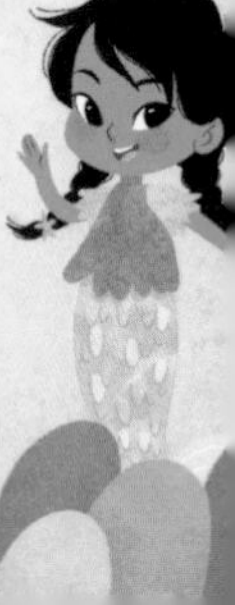

scholastic.com/acorn